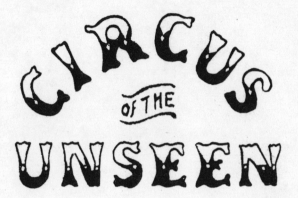

CIRCUS OF THE UNSEEN

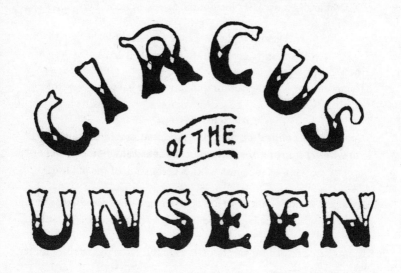

CIRCUS OF THE UNSEEN

JOANNE OWEN

HOT
KEY
BOOKS

First published in Great Britain in 2014 by Hot Key Books
Northburgh House, 10 Northburgh Street, London EC1V 0AT

Text copyright © Joanne Owen 2014
Illustration copyright © Alexis Snell 2014

A CIP catalogue record for this book is available from the British Library.

ISBN: 978-1-4714-0114-5

1

This book is typeset in 11pt Sabon using Atomik ePublisher

Printed and bound by Clays Ltd, St Ives Plc

www.hotkeybooks.com

Hot Key Books is part of the Bonnier Publishing Group
www.bonnierpublishing.com

To grandmothers, especially Edith and Thelma,
whose tales tell truths

Part One

Long ago, when the world was young and people still thought of the marsh and the mists and the witch in the woods, there lived a girl called Vasilisa, whose mother fell gravely ill. On her deathbed, Vasilisa's mother called for her daughter. She took a little wooden doll from beneath her pillow, saying, 'When I am gone, I shall leave you this doll with my blessing. Promise me you'll always keep her with you, and promise me you'll never show her to another soul. Whenever you need guidance or comfort, give the doll food and she will ease your troubles.' Vasilisa promised her mother all of these things.

When her mother died and Vasilisa felt sick with grief, she gave the doll something to eat, just as her mother had said. Then the doll's eyes shone like two stars and she told Vasilisa to lie down and rest, 'For the morning is wiser than the night.' And when Vasilisa woke, she felt some comfort, as her mother had said she would.

In time, Vasilisa's father, a merchant, sought a new wife, thinking his dear daughter deserved a mother and the companionship of women while he travelled the land doing his work, and he was overjoyed to find a woman who had two daughters of her own. But both the stepmother and

3

stepsisters were jealous of Vasilisa's beauty, and did all they could to make her life miserable. They sent her out to the fields, hoping the sun would burn her skin, and they made her work from sunrise to sundown, hoping she'd turn into a scrawny bag of bones. But each morning Vasilisa fed her doll, sometimes going without food herself, and her doll did her work until everything was done. Her stepmother and stepsisters could not understand why she never burned her skin, or became a bag of bones.

A few years passed like this and, the more tasks Vasilisa was given, the lovelier she became, while jealousy ate away at her stepmother and stepsisters like worms through a corpse. As more years passed and the merchant spent much of his time travelling away from home, his wife sold their house near the town and moved them to a miserable cottage near the forest. And right in the heart of the forest lived an old lady called Baba Yaga, who'd lived away from the world in these woods since the beginning of time. She was in the earth and the marsh, and the mists and the wind. She made the sun and the moon, and the day and the night, and all creatures were her children.

Both her appearance and habits were not of this world. Her body was a skinny bag of bones, and her teeth were like tiny, sharp knives. She flew from one place to another in a giant mortar, paddling her way with a pestle, sweeping away all trace of her path with a broom. Her hut was the only place in the forest where a fire always burned, and she was said to eat children as if they were chickens.

Every day Vasilisa's stepmother sent her deeper into the

forest, ever closer to Baba Yaga's hut, saying she needed wood, or berries, or mushrooms that could only be found in its depths, but every day Vasilisa returned unharmed, thanks to the guidance of her mother's doll. As the months passed like this, and spring became summer, and summer slipped towards autumn, the stepmother's anger became so great that she decided it was time to send Vasilisa directly into the jaws of death.

Chapter One

We'd made this journey hundreds of times, maybe thousands. We'd leave the city and turn onto smaller and smaller roads until we snaked through the village and crossed the toytown bridge to Granny's lane. I wound down the window and inhaled the smell of earth and roses, and the marshy riverbank. Those roses and that river meant we were nearly there, which meant having nothing to worry about, and everything to look forward to.

We turned onto the lane and the house came into view. First the ivy-covered walls and the upstairs windows that jutted out like bony eyebrows, then the small wooden cabin perched beside it, with the rocking horse sitting sentry by the door. It was like something from a fairy tale. I tingled. Everything was as it should be. Actually, everything was better than it should be. There was a huge moon resting on the horizon beyond the house. It looked like a massive, milky egg, pulsating with pink and silver, like a heart beating with light instead of blood. It didn't look real. It was special. *A sign*, Granny would say.

Granny was waiting outside. She rushed towards us,

smiling and waving her arms. You'd never have known she was so old. She had such soft skin, and her long hair was still autumn-red. From the back, she might have been in her twenties or thirties. She was wearing her favourite spotty green dress, which she claimed to have had since she was eighteen ('Things were made to last back then,' she said), but I noticed she had nothing on her feet, and hoped Mum hadn't seen. She was worried about Granny starting to forget things. I'd seen it a few times myself – like when we'd go to the shop and I had to remind her why we were there, or the time she forgot about the jam and it boiled over and ruined the cooker – but don't we *all* forget things? To me, she didn't seem old enough for us to be properly worried. I mean, with her looking so young, and being so full of life. Still, I'd had to promise Mum I'd look after us both before she'd let me stay on my own for the whole of the Easter holidays.

Granny practically pulled me from the car.

'I can't tell you how happy I am to see my girls,' she said, linking arms with us. 'And look at the moon! All rosy for my Rosie! Never seen it so fat. What can it mean? It must be a sign for something,' she said, which made me smile. 'Will you come in for a cup of tea before you head home, Greta?'

'I'd love to, Mum, but I should get straight back on the road. Look after each other, won't you? No mischief, and not too many late nights.'

'And you take care of yourself, my darling.' Granny hugged Mum tight. 'I do love you, you know.'

'Course.' Mum looked surprised, and I was too. I mean,

Granny was affectionate, but she and Mum didn't really use the 'L' word. 'See you in a couple of weeks.'

'Before you go, I was wondering if you'd be around tomorrow?' Granny asked. 'In case Rosie needs to call. It is her first time staying without Daisy.'

'I think Rosie's big enough to do just fine on her own, but she can call whenever she wants. See you soon, love.'

I could smell Granny's ginger and coffee cake as soon as I stepped into the hall. One of the things I loved about coming here was that it had always been the same, and it always stayed the same. Same furniture, same smells, same feeling of being warm and content even before you'd sat by the fire or scoffed any cake. Granny took hold of my hands and gave them a squeeze.

'I *have* been looking forward to having you all to myself. I love you both the same, of course, but I think I'm far too old and dotty for Daisy now she's so grown up. Promise me that won't happen to you. Promise you'll always be you.'

Unfortunately, I couldn't promise I wouldn't grow up, but I promised Granny I'd never outgrow her. I knew I could keep that one.

'But I wouldn't worry about Daisy,' I said. 'Everyone's too something or other for her. She's like Goldilocks, except with Daisy nothing's ever just right.'

I was quite pleased with myself for thinking of that, I have to admit, and it made Granny laugh too.

'You look lovely in that dress,' I told her. 'Are we going out somewhere special later? Should I get changed?'

'Thank you, Rosie, love, but you don't need a special

occasion to look nice, do you?' She smiled. 'I've always found that dressing up and looking nice makes *every* day special.'

That was one of the things that made Granny Granny. I mean, she didn't need some big reason to make an effort to look her best. And, actually, it wasn't 'making an effort' with her. That's just what she did. It was no effort at all. So we stayed in for a special night and made a pot of spicy stew together. My hand slipped with the paprika and I thought I'd ruined it, but Granny said the best ones were supposed to taste fiery. To prove it, she added another spoonful. While it simmered away, we chatted about what we'd been doing since we'd last spoken. I told her I really liked my new English teacher because she let us write our own stories, and that I thought Daisy had a boyfriend, and yes, I was still playing tennis.

'Oh, and I've been thinking about auditioning for a play.'

'How wonderful!' Granny practically whooped. 'It's been a while, hasn't it?'

'Don't get too excited. I'm not sure if I'll actually do it. I mean, I'm probably not good enough.'

'Of course you're good enough, darling. Why wouldn't you get picked? Have some faith. Besides, trying is better than doing nothing.'

'It didn't go so well last time, did it?'

I still had nightmares about that. I'd frozen on stage about a year ago. Me, the girl who'd been tipped to get a scholarship to a fancy drama school, had crumbled right in front of the director, and everyone else going for the same part. I'd started crying too, and locked myself in the toilet until Mum collected me. Humiliated doesn't get close to how crappy I felt. I fell from Promising Talent to Pathetic Failure in those eternal three minutes I was on that stage, unable to remember a word of my lines and desperate for the ground to gobble me up.

'Don't be scared of yourself, Rosie. Don't be scared of failing and, more importantly, don't be afraid of what you can do. Promise me you'll take the audition.'

'Promise,' I said, hoping I wouldn't have to break it. I knew she was right. I *shouldn't* be scared, but knowing all that didn't stop the doubting and worrying about making a fool of myself again. Then, as I laid the table, I found myself daydreaming about what I should wear to the audition. Granny had a knack for knowing how to get under my skin – in a good way, I mean.

'I haven't had goulash as good as this for years. Decades, even,' she said, and I have to say it was one of the most delicious things I'd ever eaten. 'Tastes like being bundled up in a big coat around a bonfire, don't you think? All snug and smoky. Exactly how I remember it tasting there.'

'Where?' I asked, thinking she meant a restaurant we'd been to.

'Nowhere,' she said, wiping her hands on her apron. 'Nowhere important.' But the spark in her eyes told me different.

'What's the big deal? Just tell me.'

'Perhaps you won't think it's a big deal. Perhaps you'll think it's a very tiny deal, or nothing of a deal at all.' There it was again, that naughty twinkle. She looked as if she was bursting to tell me something. 'I'm not sure I should say anything, Rosie. Your mother will be mad at me. I really shouldn't.' But then she told me her secret, which was that our goulash tasted exactly like the ones she'd eaten in Poland, where she'd lived when she was a young girl.

I had no idea she'd lived anywhere other than here, but I guess she spent so much time asking us about our lives that we never really asked much about hers. As she told me about her time there – learning the language and making friends with people who clearly became like family to her – she sparkled like nothing I'd ever seen in a person, which made me excited too.

'How long were you there?' I asked.

'Not long enough,' she said, and the spark faded a little. 'It was a dream, Rosie, an absolute dream. The bee's knees. I met my first love there too.' She fell quiet for a moment. Her brow furrowed and she clasped her neck. I'd never seen her look so serious. Then she waggled a hand, as if to wave away her words. 'I shouldn't have said anything. Your mother will be furious. It was a lifetime ago, before I had her, before I met Granddad.' She reached for a hunk of bread.

'Why did you leave?' I asked. 'It sounds like you didn't want to.'

'I had to. My mother – your great-grandmother – was very ill. I was needed at home, back here. What else could I do?' She shrugged. 'Then, because of the war, I couldn't return and, by the time it was possible to travel again, I learned that the place had been bombed and there was nothing and no one to go back to.' Her voice wavered.

'So you didn't *ever* go back?'

12

'It was bombed, Rosie. What would I be going back to?'

'But have you actually checked?' I asked. 'Maybe some people did survive. I could help you find out about them if you want. You could go back there. We could go together.' I knew I was getting carried away, but this seemed like something worth getting carried away with. I mean, it was romantic and exciting and *true*. A piece of secret history. 'Unless you check, how do you know for sure?'

'I know,' she said. 'The letters stopped coming, there was a newspaper report. It said people left the village, but even they were killed, just as they were about to cross the border into safe territory. Like I said, no survivors. Finish your food. I'm not in the mood for any more interrogation. You can't turn back what's happened. You just have to get on with it. You learn to get used to all kinds of things.'

She suddenly looked so upset, and I felt bad for going on about it. I didn't know what to say to make her feel better, so I did as she asked and finished the goulash. But I couldn't help myself. I'd seen how excited she'd been, and how much these people meant to her.

'Please tell me something else. I won't say anything to Mum. Promise.'

'You know more than you think,' she said, provocatively. 'Lots of stories I've told you came from there.'

That made sense. I mean, she used to tell me and Daisy loads of amazing fairy tales when we were small. 'Can't you tell me something else?' I asked. 'Something real?'

'All tales are real, Rosie. All tales tell truths.'

I smiled. I should have known she'd say something like

13

that. 'Tell me the tale of the man you fell in love with, then. Tell me the truth about that. What was he like? Was he why you wanted to go back?'

She stood up and straightened her dress, and I saw that her hands were shaking. She had this confused look on her face, like she didn't know what to do with herself, like she was lost.

'The answer to your question is yes,' she said. 'I wanted to go back to him. To him, and the girls.'

I followed her from the kitchen, part of me feeling guilty for pushing her to tell me more and upsetting her, but part of me dying to know more. The living room felt warm with her perfume, and it was much tidier than normal. There were usually piles of books everywhere, and pieces of material for whatever dress she was making strewn over the sofa and armchairs, but everything had been put away, and all the bookcases and ornaments looked freshly dusted. She saw that I'd noticed.

'Just been clearing away the old cobwebs,' she explained. 'Putting everything in order. Except things aren't entirely in order. I've lost a necklace. A silver necklace with a charm. Give me a hand going through these drawers, won't you? I really must find it, Rosie.'

We went through every drawer in the desk, every compartment of her sewing box, every pot and vase, but we didn't find it. Granny got down on her hands and knees and started feeling under the furniture. 'I have to find it, Rosie. I really do.'

'I'll do that,' I said, and I knelt beside her. I couldn't bear seeing her scrabbling about on the floor like that. She was frantic. 'It has to be somewhere. Why don't you make some tea and I'll look for it?'

'Make some tea? Make some tea?' she snapped. I felt crushed. Granny was never short-tempered. She was never nasty, so I guess that just showed how much she wanted to find this necklace. But she did get up and she did go to make tea and I carried on searching the room. I went through the same drawers again and again. I picked through every box of cotton reels and needles, checked on every shelf and bookcase, but still nothing, so I joined her in the kitchen. She was reading something on a piece of paper at the table. Her hands were trembling as her lips mouthed the words. When she noticed me there, she wiped her cheeks dry.

'Did you find it?'

I shook my head, silently begging her not to snap at me again. 'Not yet. Sorry. We can check the other rooms. What's wrong? Why is it so important?'

She cupped her face in her hands, and I didn't know what to do or say. I swallowed hard and asked if she needed anything. My voice came out as a whisper. I wasn't used to things being this way round. I mean, she always made *me* feel better.

'I'm sorry, Rosie. I just can't remember where I put it. It was a gift from my old friend, you see. From my Bear and the girls.' She shook her head. 'It's my own fault. I should have taken better care of it. It's frustrating. Maddening. Not knowing where things are.' She folded the paper and put it in a cake tin. 'Why don't you go and collect some eggs for us to paint? I promised Josephine we'd bring her some. I'll be all right. I'll join you in a bit. I'll just check the drawers again.'

It seemed like it might be a good idea to give her some space so I took a torch and went outside to the chicken pen, hoping she *would* be all right. I didn't want to see her cry again. The pen was at the side of the house, next to the cabin. Mum hated the chickens. She said Granny had decided to get them around the same time she started to forget things, but it seemed to me that they were good for her. They meant she wasn't on her own so much. I mean, I know they're only chickens, but they gave her something to look after. Granny once told me she kept them near her cabin in case she needed to borrow their legs and run away, because you never knew when you might need to make a quick escape. This had made me giggle, but now all I could think about was the people she'd left behind in Poland. What if some of her friends *had* survived? There had to be a way to find out, to know for sure.

I'd collected about a half a dozen eggs when Granny came out, holding the cake tin.

'That's plenty. Let's go to the cabin. The paints are in there somewhere, and we can make all the mess we want, and then hunt for the eggs, like when you were little.'

The cabin was another thing I loved about coming here. I guess it had started out as a shed but had been transformed into what I imagined a cosy Alpine chalet was like. The windows had specially made shutters painted forest-green and mustardy yellow, and the inside walls were covered in tapestries of woods and animals. There was no electricity, but it had a real fireplace.

I found the paint and we decorated the eggs with bright

16

swirls and flowers. Daisy and I used to do this every Easter, but doing it now without her, after all this time, made me realise how much things had changed now she was older. I missed her. We used to know everything about each other. We used to share secrets.

Once the eggs had dried, Granny told me to close my eyes while she hid them. I'd hardly had a chance to close them when I heard her banging around the room. She was rummaging through a cabinet, all frantic about the necklace again. I could see her breath in the air. I suggested we go back to the house. 'I'll check every room,' I promised. 'Let's go – it's freezing in here.'

She shook her head. 'I'll light a fire. It's time for a fire. I can't wait any longer.'

She knelt in the hearth. There were two nests of Russian dolls there – four round-bellied sisters, laid out in a row. There should have been six, but the smallest of each set had been missing for as long as I can remember. Daisy and I used to play house with them, pretend to feed them tea and cake. Each doll had the words *For DR, for our girls* carved into its base. The 'DR' were Granny's initials – for Dorothy Rose, the same name as mine. Daisy had been named after Dad's mum, and me after Granny, although I'd always been called Rosie. Granny sealed the dolls back inside each other and handed both sets to me, saying one was for me and one was for Daisy, and that we should keep them safe because they'd looked after her, and now they'd look after us, like Vasilisa's doll looked after her in the story.

'What story?' I asked.

'You don't remember it?' She sounded offended. I really didn't remember it, which made me feel guilty, but she'd told me so many.

'What's it about?' I asked.

'You should read it again for yourself,' she said. 'It's one of the best. As I always say, all tales have truths, Rosie, but especially that one.'

With help from a pair of bellows, Granny got the fire going really quickly and we knelt in front of it, rubbing our hands and leaning in far too close to warm our cheeks. After a while, she patted my knee and said I should take some eggs to Josephine. Then she looked at me with these big, wide eyes.

'I love you, my darling,' she said. 'You'll be just fine, you know. And you really shouldn't be afraid of that audition,' she added. 'It's wrong to let fear stop you doing what you need to do. That won't get you anywhere. Always stay strong. Always stay true to who you are, Greta. Always stay true to what you want.'

'I'm Rosie.'

'What?' She looked confused and lost, all twitchy and fidgeting with her fingers.

'I'm Rosie. You called me Greta.'

'I know who you are,' she snapped again. 'Take these eggs.' She handed me three.

'Isn't it too late?' I asked. 'Can't it wait until the morning?'

'It's not even seven yet. Off you go, and don't forget your dolls.'

'I won't be long. I can leave the dolls here.'

I put the eggs in my pocket and left quickly, blinking back

tears. I didn't want her to see she'd upset me, and I didn't want to upset her any further. I shouldn't have picked her up on saying the wrong name.

The air was sharp and made my eyes sting. It smelled like snow was coming, and the moon looked different now. It was a grubby lemon colour, with pinky-grey patches smudged across it. Everything felt smudged. I knew saying the wrong name didn't *have* to mean anything bad. It's easy to get people's names muddled up, isn't it? Mum often called me Daisy by mistake. But that wasn't all, that wasn't everything. I was also worried by the way she was being so snippy with me, and angry with herself.

I walked as far as the village green, and stopped. Josephine, Granny's oldest friend, lived just the other side of it, only another five minutes away, but I suddenly felt terrible about leaving Granny. I had to get back. I started to walk home, then picked up speed until I was actually running. Weirdly, the dolls were sitting just outside the cabin when I got there. Maybe she was annoyed I hadn't taken them with me. I picked them up and went to open the door. It was locked.

'Granny? Are you still there?'

She didn't answer. I went to the window. The shutters were closed, and I could smell burning. There was smoke coming from under the cabin door.

'Granny!' I screamed.

I threw down the dolls, pulled on the handle and kicked at the door, but nothing made any difference. It felt like it was bolted from the inside. I ran to the house and called 999 from Granny's landline and rushed back to the cabin. The chickens were flapping and screeching and I could hardly breathe for all the smoke. It wasn't long before the fire engine came, and then the whole village. I watched, everyone watched, as the firemen battered down the cabin door and stormed inside. I rushed after them, but Josephine dragged me back by my coat.

I was shaking like mad when I gathered up the dolls, and I saw that the moon was just a great big dirty smear in the sky. I couldn't get that lost look on her face out of my head.

Chapter Two

I don't know how long I'd been there, but sometime later Mum, Dad and Daisy came to Josephine's. Mum was in an awful state. She came at me like a crazy person and asked me over and over again if I was all right. When she eventually let go of me, she begged me to tell her how it had happened, what we were doing in the cabin.

How could it have happened, Rosie? How could it? Why did you leave her?

I couldn't say anything. I just sat there, listening to her words, but not really feeling anything. Dad tried to get Mum to have a lie-down but she wouldn't, she couldn't. Then Dad told me I shouldn't feel bad about leaving Granny alone, that it was an accident, and there was nothing anyone could have done. I knew he was saying that to make me feel better, but I also knew I could have done something, and I knew I shouldn't have left her there. We should have gone back to the house, or we should have both gone to Josephine's. I fetched my coat.

'We painted these for you.' I gave Josephine the eggs, then I gave Daisy her set of dolls, and I started to cry. At some point Dad carried me up to bed, but I didn't sleep. I spent all night beating myself up for leaving her, but not just that. I also couldn't stop thinking about all that stuff she'd said about living in Poland, and how crazy she'd gone looking for the necklace. I guessed it was from the man she'd fallen in love with there. He had to be her 'Bear'. Maybe she'd been missing him all this time and had never said. Maybe she'd kept it bottled up all these years, and then tidying up and remembering the necklace had brought it all out. I didn't know, and now I never would.

We stayed with Josephine while Dad sorted out the funeral. Those days passed in numbness. No one said very much, and most of what was said was about the 'arrangements'. We were detached from what had happened, and each other, but at least Mum was calmer.

The night before the funeral, Mum and Dad said I didn't have to go, but I did. As much as I was scared of it, I had to be there. I was up and dressed far too early, but didn't want to go downstairs, because that meant it was starting to happen, and I didn't want to feel it happening, because that would make it true. I felt numb and jittery at the same time, suspended between everything. Nothing felt real. Nothing could exist until today was over. I went to the window. There was a thin, sparkly layer of frost covering the green. Almost snow. Whenever it snowed, Granny said it was Lady Snowstorm shaking her skirts from her house in the clouds. She would have loved how it looked right now. We would have made a snowman today. It would have been tiny, but we would have made one.

'Can I come in, love?' It was Mum. 'The cars will be here soon. You should come down, try to eat something.' She rubbed my arm, and I went down with her, but I couldn't eat. I sipped some tea and then Dad came to say the cars were waiting.

I was almost sick when I saw the coffin. There she was, only a metre from me, but so far away. I pictured her lying just the other side of the wood. I knew she was wearing that spotty dress, and I knew she had a penny in her pocket. Dad said she'd need a penny to pay the boatman for her passing. He said that was the thing to do. The box was so small. I'd never noticed she was so small. Seeing it made everything more real and less real at the same time. Seeing it was absurd. I mean, seeing that we end up in a little box was mad-crazy absurd.

Daisy and I held hands all the way to the church and all through the service, and I knew it was nearly over when I saw a blur of orange through the windows, which made me feel sick again, because I knew why the people wearing those fluorescent coats were there – they were the grave diggers. We went outside in the wind and stood over the frosty hole in the earth. And though it was cold, my head was hot and my hands were sweaty, and I started to think about all the other people here. All the dead people, and all the people around Granny's grave. All the lives people had lived, and all the lives people were still trying to live. And I imagined I could hear inside everyone's head, and see everything that made them the person they were, and I felt like I was floating and sinking, all at the same time.

When the words had been said, when we were supposed to leave the orange-coat-men to tuck her in with the earth, I took one of the dolls from the set Granny had given me and dropped it into her grave so she'd have something to look after her. I kept the other doll safe in my pocket. Then we filed away, and I was shaking so much Daddy put his arm around me and practically carried me back to the car. I hated leaving her there, all alone in that box. We just left her there, like I'd left her alone in the cabin.

Everyone went back to Josephine's for tea. I didn't feel like eating, but Mum said I should have something, and handed me a tiny cherry pie. As I bit into it, I found myself smiling about one of Granny's stories. It was about a girl, a bear and a basket of pies. *Mashenka and the Beast Who Walked Like a Man*, I think it was called. I must have been about five or six when she first told me that story and managed to turn a day to remember for all the wrong reasons into a day to remember for a better reason. I'd been riding my bike up and down the lane when a bigger boy turned up and threw something at me. I remember braking hard as it hit the spokes, and then almost flying over the handlebars. Then I saw the thing slither away so fast I hardly had time to see it. But I did see it – a skinny grey snake – and I'd never been so scared.

I dumped the bike, ran to the nearest tree and scrambled up as quickly as I could, thinking there was no way a snake could climb a tree and get me there. The boy stood there, laughing at me, and the worse thing was, I couldn't hide my face or tell him to go away or anything. I couldn't move.

I was frozen there, terrified of being up so high, terrified that making one tiny move would send me plummeting to the ground. After a while, Granny came looking for me. The boy ran off and she had to climb up the tree, prise my fingers off, one by one, and do a lot of talking to get me down.

When I was back on the ground and told her what had happened, she didn't tell me off for being silly and making her climb a tree, and she didn't tell me off for making things up because there weren't any snakes in this part of the world. She listened, and she believed that I believed the boy had thrown a snake at me. Then she took my hand and led me down to the room in her cellar and told me a story about a brave, clever girl called Mashenka, who was taken captive by a bear, the Beast Who Walked Like a Man. Mashenka begged him to let her take a basket of pies to feed her poor parents. Of course, the beast refused to let her go, but he agreed to take them himself, so Mashenka hid herself in the basket and the beast unwittingly brought her home.

I remember asking Granny if she thought I could be like Mashenka, and she told me I already was a brave girl, and that one little thing like what had just happened didn't mean anything. But I told her I wasn't really very brave because I could never play on the lane again in case that boy was there and did it again, or laughed at me for crying.

'Of course you could,' she said, and told me I should never let what other people thought stop me from doing what I wanted. But, she added, if I ever felt scared again, we could come to our cave in the cellar and feel safe, because nothing could hurt us here, not even bigger boys or skinny snakes.

Now we were here, at Josephine's, I wanted to go to Granny's cellar right then, not hurting, and not feeling scared about how I'd manage without her. But I couldn't just leave, and I knew she wouldn't be there, so I just concentrated hard on what she'd said about being brave, and asked Daddy if he'd get everyone to do a toast to her. He gave me a hug and pinged a knife on a glass and said we should raise our glasses to Granny. I sipped some wine, then gulped down the rest of the glass and felt really dizzy. Mum must have noticed because she came over and fed me more pie and told me how much I reminded her of her mum. I couldn't bear it any longer, so I ran outside to be on my own, but a few minutes later I felt someone behind me. It was Mum. She squeezed me so hard it hurt.

'At least she told you she loved you before it happened,' I said into Mum's hair. And then I remembered what she'd said to me too, before I left the cabin. *I love you, my darling. You'll be just fine, you know.* It was like she'd said goodbyes to us both.

Chapter Three

A few months later we made that same journey again. But this wasn't like any of the others. This wasn't a quick visit for tea, or lunch, or for the holidays. This was for good. The car swerved off the road onto the lane and my head smacked against the window. There was blood, and I knew there'd be a bump the size of an egg tomorrow. I wound down the window and inhaled the smell of earth and roses, and the marshy riverbank. At least they were the same as they'd always been. But while they were the same, nothing else was, because when we arrived, Granny wouldn't be there, because Granny was gone.

'Close it. I'm freezing.'

I did as I was told. Daisy always got what she wanted. That's how it was. I wiped smears of blood from the glass.

'I'm definitely having the big bedroom upstairs, aren't I, Mum?' Daisy asked, actually pouting. 'If you're forcing me to live in this dead-end ghost town, I need something as compensation, don't you think? I mean, what am I actually going to *do* here? I still don't understand why we had to move. I know you and Granny were born here, and I know the house is bigger, but I don't want to be stuck here, trapped like –'

'Stop it, Daisy.' Dad caught her eye in the mirror. 'You might actually come to like it.'

I said nothing, and Mum said nothing. We watched the house come into view, and then the charred cabin. Mum caught my eye. We both looked away, and Mum concentrated on pretending to look for something in her bag, while I concentrated on counting how many different kinds of birds were in the garden. I'd got to four when I noticed a jumble of boxes and furniture stacked up outside the house.

'What's that stuff doing there?' I asked. 'You can't throw it away. That's her life.'

'They're just things, Rosie,' Mum almost snapped. 'Things aren't a person's life.'

'I know. I didn't mean . . .' It came out all gruff and I broke off. Mum was already walking down the path, kicking out at the leaves like they'd done something to make her really angry, but it was me who'd done that.

'You're not *really* getting rid of Granny's stuff, are you, Dad?' I asked. 'What about all her books?'

'Now's not the time, love. And go easy on Mum, eh? She needs a bit of time to get used to things.'

'That's exactly why we shouldn't do anything rash like chucking all her stuff away,' I shouted after him. 'It's too soon.' I couldn't believe they'd done this without saying anything. It looked like Granny had been thrown out of her own house. Was I the only one who cared? I knew Mum was right about things not being a person's life, but

28

wiping out someone's entire physical presence seemed totally disrespectful.

I hung back by the car until they'd all gone through the front door. I'd been terrified of going back inside the house nearly as much as going to the funeral, but it was something I had to do on my own. I gripped the iron door handle. *One, two, three*, I counted, and stepped into the hall. I opened my eyes. It still looked the same here. Chequered tiles on the floor, mirror by the coat stand, and the photo of me and Daisy at an old-fashioned steam fair next to that. We were holding hands, grinning like mad things in front of a lorry that had the words 'Relive Grandma's Yesterday' painted on the side in swirly letters. But while everything looked the same, it didn't smell quite the same, and that made me feel all wrong, like I'd been sawn in half by a magician, and the two halves had been separated. I know that sounds dumb, but what I mean is that half of me felt like I always did when I came here, and the other half didn't know where it was.

'Stop admiring yourself.' Daisy came up behind me and stuck out her tongue at the mirror. 'You're not as pretty as you think.'

'But I wasn't, and I don't . . .'

'Stop arguing,' called Mum. 'Leave those boxes in the kitchen and try to get some of your stuff unpacked before dinner. You know where your rooms are.'

Yep, Daisy was *definitely* having the big room upstairs and I was having the room in the cellar. It hadn't been easy to persuade Mum to let me, though. She was right, it was cold down there, and I had to crouch to get into bed because the ceiling curved so low, and it was two floors away from the other bedrooms, but that's why I wanted it. That's what had made it our secret cave. Almost all Granny's furniture had been replaced with mine, apart from the dressing table and an armchair, but it smelled the same as ever, of her warm, sandalwood perfume. The horrible thing was, being here right now wasn't making me feel safe or like nothing could hurt me. It was making me hurt.

I flopped onto the bed and pulled the covers over my head, but kept imagining Granny creaking down the stairs and surprising me with a mug of something hot and sweet, so I got up and finished unpacking.

I thought Mum and Dad had cleared everything out, but in the bottom drawer of the dressing table, right at the back, I found a parcel tied with string. I opened it and saw a flash of silver. My heart flipped. A silver necklace, with a charm – this had to be Granny's necklace, the one she'd gone crazy trying to find. I sat at the dressing table and fastened it round my neck. The bear-shaped charm sat high on my throat. It had tiny rubies for eyes. It was beautiful, really unique. And then I started thinking about what would have happened if we'd looked here and found it. Maybe she wouldn't have got upset, and then maybe, I don't know, maybe it wouldn't have happened.

The necklace wasn't the only thing in the package. There were also two pairs of babies' shoes – one red, the other green – a couple of letters and an old photo of Granny. She must have been about twenty, and she was wearing *that* dress, the dotty one, and she had a ribbon in her hair.

I swallowed hard. Her smile was exactly the same, that wide grin that made her whole face sparkle. She seemed so happy. She was standing outside a hut that looked a lot like the cabin here, but there were mountains behind it, and a lake to the side. It must have been taken *there*, in Poland. I guessed the letters were from the man she'd wanted to go back to. They were written in what must have been Polish and signed off with an undecipherable squiggle. I wished I could read what they said. I remembered the look on her face that showed how much she missed these people, and now I knew how that felt for myself.

I knew Granny had said Mum didn't like her talking about her past, but everything was different now. Maybe she would be interested in this stuff. Maybe she knew about these people. I climbed back into bed, actually feeling excited about having this chance to find out more about Granny's life, and I knew I had to think about doing something with my own too. It bugged me that I never did take that audition, which meant I still had a promise to honour. But, at that moment, I just wanted to throw everything into looking at Granny's past.

Chapter Four

I heard the front door banging shut, Dad and Daisy's voices outside and then the car leaving. I sat bolt upright, remembering the stuff I'd found last night. I had to talk to Mum about it. I got dressed, grabbed Granny's things and went upstairs.

'Fancy boiled egg and soldiers?' I called to Mum.

'Lovely, thanks Rosie.'

Mum came down in her dressing gown, looking like she'd hardly slept. I couldn't remember what she'd been like when Granddad died. I was too young. I think he'd been ill for ages, so it wasn't such a shock. I didn't know how she'd coped with him dying, but I did know that Granny being gone had really changed Mum. She'd been distant ever since.

I reached for a toast soldier and knocked over the salt. Mum picked up a few grains and threw them over her shoulder. 'Had enough bad luck, haven't we?' she said.

'What do you mean?'

'The old wives' tale, you know? Spilling salt is meant to bring bad luck, so you're supposed to throw some over your shoulder to stop it, to blind the devil or something.'

She brushed her hands. 'What are those shoes doing on the table?'

'I wanted to ask you about them. They were in a package at the back of my dressing table. Are they mine and Daisy's?'

She looked them over. 'They look handmade, lovely leather, but definitely not yours.'

'They were with these letters, and this photo of Granny.' I showed her. 'Look at her dress. She's wearing that same dress. It must have been taken when she went abroad. She told me she lived in Poland and only came back here because her mum was ill. Do you know *exactly* where she lived in Poland? Do you know anything about the people she met there? Did you know about any of this?'

Mum took the photo. The way her breath quickened when she looked at it made me think she'd seen it before, that she did know something.

'What is it, Mum? What do you know?'

'Nothing.' She sniffed and laid the photo face down on the table. 'I can't help you, Rosie.'

'But it's amazing, don't you think? All these things we never knew about Granny. And don't you think the building in the photo looks like the cabin? Maybe she built it to remind her of that place.'

'I don't know. Like I said, I can't help you.'

I rapped my spoon against the egg cup. I felt like I was hitting my head against a wall. Why was Mum being so difficult? It was like trying to reason with Daisy.

'Are you sure you can't remember anything else? And don't you want to know more?' I asked. 'I mean, some of the things Granny told me just before she . . . she died, and now finding this stuff?'

'The past is best left alone, love. You're not always better off knowing everything, believe me. Fancy a walk?' she asked, changing the subject. 'Dad was dropping Daisy in the village. We could catch her up. We could see if there's a theatre group here. I know you were thinking of taking that audition. It would be good for you, love.'

Maybe Mum was right; maybe it would do me good to join something here.

But I didn't care about that right now. All I wanted was to know what the letters said. I wanted to know what *all* this stuff meant, and why Mum was being so cagey. It was obvious she knew more than she was letting on, and her being all secretive was only making me determined to know more. Whatever it was, it clearly *was* a big deal, to Mum as well as to Granny. And I thought I knew where to start: I wanted to read that story Granny had mentioned, the one about Vasilisa and the dolls, the one she'd said was the most important story of all. I felt for my doll in my pocket. I hadn't been without it since that night.

'I'll stay here,' I said. 'I was thinking of tidying up around the cabin.'

'You don't have to bother yourself with that, Rosie. I've arranged for someone to clear everything away. It's being pulled down next week. We need to get on with our lives. It's for the best.'

I turned cold. It was too soon.

'Don't you want to remember her?' As the words slipped

from my mouth, I knew how awful they sounded. 'Sorry.'

'I don't want a constant reminder of how she died.' Mum froze. She was staring at me like I'd done something terrible. 'Where did you get that?'

'This?' I touched the necklace. 'It was with the other stuff I found in my room. This is what Granny was looking for that night. She was desperate to find it. She said it was from someone she loved. Have you seen it before? Isn't it –?'

'You have to stop this, Rosie. I can't live in the past.'

'Wanting to know about the past isn't the same as living in it.'

'Please. Go to your room.'

I did as she asked, but I wasn't letting this go. I didn't yet know what the big secret was, but I had to find out. I was *going to* find out.

Chapter Five

I waited in my room until I heard Mum leave. She slammed the door so hard the windows shook. Why had she gone so mad-crazy at me about the necklace? It wasn't my fault Granny had loved someone else before she met Granddad, if that's what had upset her. I knew Granny was her mother, but she was my grandmother. Mum didn't have *all* the rights over her. This was as much my history as hers.

My head felt a bit clearer once I was outside. It was one of those mornings that make you feel like you're stepping into a brand new world. I mean, the smell of the air, and the bright light and the pink flowers bursting through the earth. Everything seemed clean. But there were no flowers around the cabin. The earth was all scorched, and just seeing it, being that close to it, made me feel sick. I couldn't bring myself to go inside. Not yet.

I decided to tidy the chicken pen instead. It was in a right state, a jungle of weeds and old straw and mess, and no chickens. I panicked. THERE WERE NO CHICKENS. Crap. I hadn't thought about what had happened to them. Maybe Josephine had taken them. I *hoped* Josephine had taken them.

I swept the soggy straw from the run, then leaned into the coop and scooped out a bundle of bedding. It was full of rotting flesh and feathers and bone and shards of broken shell. I threw it back down, trying not to retch. They'd either starved to death and rotted, or maybe a fox had got in. Or maybe it was the fire. They were too messed up to tell.

I put on gloves, swept it all up and pushed it into a bin bag, as best as I could without actually looking at what I was handling. I was about to go back to the house when I noticed the cabin door had blown open – just a little, but enough for me to see into the room. This was the kind of thing Granny would have said was a sign. I had to go in, didn't I? If Mum really was going to have it pulled down, I didn't have much time to see if anything could be salvaged. I took a deep breath, and forced myself to step over the threshold.

Inside, it looked like an ancient shipwreck, precarious, and burned back to its crumbling skeleton. The floor and remains of the furniture were covered in what looked like a dusting of black snow. The walls were covered in bubbles that turned to powder when I touched them. All the tapestries were gone, all the colour and life. I could make out the fireplace though, and all I could see was me and Granny warming our hands, her in that dress, snapping at me, and then me leaving her on her own.

I flipped round to the door. There were voices just outside.

'Did you know your house is supposed to be haunted?' A girl's head appeared in the opening. 'Must be *extra* haunted now.' She sniggered. 'Burned like a proper witch, didn't she?'

'Leave it, Amy,' said a boy. Luke, I think his name was.

I recognised him from when we'd stayed here last summer. He'd hung around Daisy the whole time. I guessed the girl was his sister.

'What do you want?' I asked. 'Daisy's not here.'

Luke looked embarrassed. 'Don't listen to her,' he said, glancing at his sister. 'She's an idiot.'

'You're the idiot. She's an idiot. You're both idiots.' The girl gave me a filthy look and left, which was just as well. I had a massive urge to punch her. Not that I would have, but the urge was definitely there.

Luke took a step inside and brushed against a wall. There were powdery traces on his sleeve, and I really wanted to wipe them off him. I didn't want anyone to have a single piece of this place. 'Sorry about my sister,' he said. 'And sorry about your gran. She was a nice lady.'

Neither of us said anything for what felt like an age, but he eventually broke the awkward silence. 'I meant what I said about your gran. She was a legend.'

That didn't exactly help with the awkwardness. It felt weird hearing a stranger talk about her. 'How do you know?' I asked. 'What do you know about her?'

'I know she put me in my place when I threw that worm at you.'

'That was you? A worm? I thought it was a snake.' I immediately regretted mentioning that. Of course it wasn't a snake, and now I felt like an idiot. The funny thing was it made me feel better to know that the person who'd done that to me was just this gangly, nervous boy, and nothing at all to be scared of.

'She said if I ever did anything like that ever again, all the worms in the world would turn into snakes and come and find me. Then she gave me a sweet and told me she was joking.' He laughed. 'But I haven't gone near a worm since.'

'You deserved it.' I laughed too, and he stepped right inside and had a good look round.

'What are you doing in here, anyway?'

'I really wanted to clean it up. My mum wants to get rid of it, but I . . . I don't know. I wanted to see if it could be fixed up, see if anything could be saved.'

I didn't know why I was telling him all these things. I hardly knew him. Actually, *that* was probably the reason. I didn't know him, and he didn't really know Granny, so he wasn't going to get all upset and make me feel even worse when I was trying to make things better by talking about her. That's what kept happening with Mum. It always ended in tears, or an argument, or both.

'I'll help, if you like. Not sure there's anything left to save, but we could clean it up.'

I didn't know what to say. I mean, I didn't think I could do it alone, but I wasn't sure it was right to let a stranger help me.

'We should start with the big stuff.' Luke began heaping all the larger furniture into one part of the cabin, so I just got on with it too. Once we'd carried all that outside, we fetched a load of bin bags and swept up all the smaller bits. After a couple of hours it was pretty much tidy, except for around the hearth. I'd left that until last, because that was the hardest, because I knew she'd been found near there. I moved the bellows aside and picked up the coal scuttle. It was much heavier than I'd expected. As I tried to heave it away, it slipped from my grip and broke right through the floor. The area around it fell away and a deep hole opened up.

'Look at this.' I waved him over. 'It's really weird. There's a massive gap down here.'

'What? Like a secret passageway?'

I knelt and reached into the hole. 'Don't know. I can't feel where it ends. Maybe . . .' I shut myself up. 'Stop making fun of me.'

'I wasn't, actually. Well, not *exactly*.'

I leaned into the hole again and saw a glimmer of silver and red. It was Granny's cake tin. I opened it. There was a slab of mouldy ginger cake inside, and a folded-up piece of paper with Mum's name written on it in Granny's spidery handwriting. I'd seen her put this in the tin. I opened it, curious to know what she'd been reading in the kitchen that night.

My darling Greta,

I've written so many versions of this note, none of them right. But here it is, as it is, the best I could do, because you deserve to know the truth, my darling, so I shall just say it. The fire was no accident. It was my doing, my decision, my wish. I don't expect forgiveness for the hurt this will cause, but I hope with all my heart that you can come to understand why I had to end my life in this world.

You are a mother, Greta. You can imagine the pain of having to leave your young daughters, and the horror of learning you will never see them again. *Imagine trying to live with the fact that you weren't there to protect them when they needed you most. Imagine the agony of never having the chance to say a real goodbye. Imagine that pain, Greta, and multiply it over and over, for mine has worsened as time has passed to the point where I can bear it no more. I need to return to the family I left and lost a lifetime ago. I understand why you were unable to accept them, of course I do, and now I ask you to try to understand why I have chosen to go.*

The life we've shared has brought me so much joy, my darling, but I am old. My mind isn't what it was, I'm not who I was and my heart can hold no more pain. The time has come for me to cross the threshold from this life to what lies beyond. It is time for me to join those I left behind, my Bear and my girls, my Anastazja and Lilka. But I leave this world thankful for the life I have been lucky to lead, and calm in the knowledge that it is my time to pass.

I wish your girls, darling Daisy and Rosie, the world. I have left my dolls for them, to see them through their lives. And Greta, my girl, I thank you for making my world so special and seeing me through my life.

Your loving mother.

Part of me wished I'd never read it, but most of me felt like I'd been torn up into tiny pieces. It couldn't be right. I mean, I *had* to be reading it wrong. But as I reread Granny's words, over and over, with my heart burning and my head spinning, and they kept saying the same thing, there was no getting away from it. Granny had *meant* to die. It was there, in scribbly black and white. That's why she'd made me go to Josephine's, that's why she'd wanted me to take the dolls, that's why she'd 'cleared away the cobwebs'. It was all planned out, and I'd let it happen. I'd left her alone to do it.

And she'd had a family before Mum. Two secret daughters who'd died, and she'd left us for them . . .

My head was spinning so much I lost my balance and fell forward, into the hole.

And I just kept falling.

All I could hear was inside my own head, and all I could see was inside my head. The earth had swallowed me up.

Part Two

One autumn night when the leaves fell thick and the frost bit hard, Vasilisa's stepmother conspired with her daughters to get rid of Vasilisa for good. She gave all three girls a task. The eldest was told to make lace, the middle girl was told to knit stockings and Vasilisa, the youngest, was told to spin wool. The stepmother went to bed, leaving one candle alight for the girls to finish their work by. As the night went on, the eldest sister went to the candle and pretended to straighten the wick. She put out the flame and, feigning alarm, said that someone would have to go to Baba Yaga's hut to fetch more fire. 'But not I,' she said, 'for I can see by the light of my pins.'

'And not I,' said the middle sister, 'for I can see by the light of my needles.'

'Then that's settled,' said the eldest. 'Vasilisa must go.' And they pushed her out into the night.

Vasilisa sat on the doorstep and fed her doll, wondering what she should do, for she was frightened of making the journey alone. Once she was fed, the doll's eyes shone like two stars and she told Vasilisa to go, promising she would be protected. A little way along the path, a horseman galloped by. He was dressed in white, and his horse was white and, as he passed, dawn broke. A little further along the path, a second horseman galloped by. He was dressed in red, his horse was red and, as he passed, the sun rose.

Vasilisa walked on through the day and eventually came to Baba Yaga's hut. The sight of it filled her with dread. It had a fence made of bones, there were skulls on the fence posts and the door had a human mouth in place of a lock. As Vasilisa stood there, shaking with fear, a third horseman galloped by. He was dressed in black, and his horse was black and, as he rode up to Baba Yaga's door and vanished, night fell. Just then, the skulls on the fence posts glowed through the darkness and fire flamed from their eye sockets and it became as bright as day. The trees crackled and creaked and all the leaves rustled and Baba Yaga emerged from the woods, sailing the sky in a mortar, sweeping away all traces of her path with a broom.

'Who goes there?' said Baba Yaga, sniffing the air. 'I smell human blood!'

'It's Vasilisa,' she said. 'My stepsisters sent me to fetch light.'

'I know them,' said Baba Yaga, for she knew most things. 'But before I give you light, you must work for me and, if you fail in your tasks, I shall eat you up, spit out your bones and burn them!'

They went inside and Baba Yaga ordered Vasilisa to serve her the food cooking on the stove. There was enough to feed a dozen people, but Baba Yaga gobbled everything down, except for a drop of cabbage soup, a crust of bread and a scrap of pork rind. Then she gave Vasilisa her tasks. She *was to sweep the yard, clean the hut, wash the bedclothes, sort through a great pile of wheat and cook dinner before the next day was out. 'If you don't,' Baba Yaga warned, 'I shall eat you up, spit out your bones and burn them!'*

Once Baba Yaga had settled down for the night and the cottage shook with her snores, Vasilisa offered her doll the leftover food and asked what she should do, fearing the work was impossible for a person to get through in a single day. But the doll said she'd already eaten her fill and needed no more and, with her eyes shining like two stars, she told Vasilisa to rest, 'For the morning is wiser than the night.'

Next morning, Vasilisa rose as the light from the skulls was fading. The White Rider galloped by, day broke and Baba Yaga went outside. She whistled and her mortar, pestle and broom appeared. Then the Red Rider galloped by and the sun rose, and Baba Yaga climbed into her mortar and took flight. Vasilisa looked around, saw that her work had already been done, and thanked her doll for delivering her from death.

That evening the Black Rider came, the night fell, the skulls' eyes glowed through the darkness, and Baba Yaga came from the woods. When she saw that Vasilisa had done everything she'd asked she exploded in rage, angry she had nothing to complain about.

'Why don't you speak, child?' asked Baba Yaga. 'Have you lost your tongue?'

'I don't dare,' replied Vasilisa. 'But, if I'm allowed, I'd like to ask one question.'

'Then ask, child,' said Baba Yaga. 'But not every question

has a good answer, and if you ask too much, and know too much, you'll grow old before your time.'

'Who are the three riders?' asked Vasilisa.

'They are my day and my sun and my night, child. They are my faithful servants,' Baba Yaga replied, and then she asked if Vasilisa had any more questions.

Vasilisa shook her head. 'You said if a person asks too much, and knows too much, they'll grow old faster, and I don't want to grow old faster.'

'Very good,' Baba Yaga replied. 'You paid attention.' Then she asked Vasilisa how she'd managed to get all the work done. Remembering the promise she'd made to her mother, Vasilisa kept her doll hidden away in her pocket, and said it was due to her mother's blessing.

'I'll have no blessed ones in my house!' shrieked Baba Yaga, and she dragged Vasilisa outside, stuck a skull on a stick and passed it to her. 'Here, take this for your stepsisters. This is what they sent you for, and may they enjoy it! Now begone!'

And Vasilisa ran home through the forest by the light of the glowing skull.

Chapter Six

I woke up screaming. I'd never felt such pain. It was like shards of ice were stabbing into my head. I rolled onto my side, clutching Granny's doll. The ground was damp against my bare legs, and I could smell wet earth. The last thing I remembered was being in the cabin with that boy. And after that, then what? Nothing. There was nothing in my head about what had happened until this. I pushed myself up. Every movement sent another stab into my head, and my whole body was sore.

Daddy? Mum? I called. No answer. Nothing. A sliver of moon slipped out from the clouds. There was crumbling stonework all around me, stretching out as far as I could see. I couldn't catch my breath, I was frozen to the spot, in the middle of a graveyard. But I hadn't walked here myself, so how was it possible?

I had to get out, but I couldn't see a path. It was completely overgrown, no flowers, no well-tended graves. I started to weave my way through them, looking for a gate, for any way out, for any end to it. I picked up speed and stumbled into a statue of a girl. I could see her face clearly in the silver light.

Her expression looked real, and her hands reached out as if she was offering me a gift of the dead leaves cupped in them.

I pulled back the twisted branches and briars to read the inscription. This was crazy. I traced my fingers over the letters. I was right. They spelled out my name, Granny's name, our name – but this wasn't Granny's grave. I felt my heart twist itself into a tiny, spiky ball and I ran and I ran and I just kept going.

After a while, I came to a grove. The ground was soft and springy underfoot, like expensive carpet, and the air smelled sweet. I snaked through the lush trees and found myself in a clearing. At its centre was an old-fashioned carousel with a red-and-white striped canopy.

'Hello?' I called. 'Anyone there?' I heard my voice echo back at me. But no one answered. I noticed a booth on the edge of the carousel platform. It had to be the control room or maybe a ticket office. I ran to it, wondering if there might be a phone there, maybe even an attendant. It was too dark to see anything clearly, but there was no sign of anything electrical like a phone, and definitely no attendant.

A deafening beating sound started up, and dozens of shiny black birds surged from the trees and swept around the carousel. The first looked like crows, but those that came after were huge, prehistoric-looking creatures, with stony, blue-grey beaks as long as swords. Shaking with fear, I ducked down and watched them soar round and round, gaining height with each revolution. Their claws looked strong enough to pick me up, and sharp enough to tear me to pieces. It started snowing too. It fell thick and fast and the birds vanished into it.

I waited a few minutes, to be certain they really had gone, before I left the booth. I grabbed onto a pole to pull myself aboard the platform. It had carvings coiled around it, snake-like creatures with dragons' heads and eggs for eyes, and the platform was carpeted with dewy grass. It felt like a living thing, like the grass was actually growing there.

A clanging musical sound started up, a cross between an oompah band and a knackered ice-cream van. It swelled louder and faster and turned into a full-on polka tune. I heard a snapping noise above me. A series of shutters were opening around the outer edge of the striped canopy. Behind each was a lantern that cast flickering light over the rides. There were horses and hares, and a boar and a bear. There were foxes and goats, and leopards and wolves. Then a spotlight flicked on over the centre of the carousel, illuminating a woman's back.

'Where am I?' I asked, rushing towards her. 'Where is this?' She was seated at a large spinning wheel, wild-haired and sitting straight as a broom handle, her arms reaching out to the spindle rooted into the platform. She didn't reply. She just pumped her foot on the pedal at the base of the wheel's framework and the carousel started to move, slowly at first, but it wasn't long before it was rolling and creaking like an old ship in a storm, rising and falling in juddering waves while the animals moved up and down their snaky poles.

I tapped her shoulder. She felt hard, solid as wood. My heart sank. This wasn't a woman at all. This was a mechanical doll, with six eyes staring out from her three faces. One was smooth and young looking, with cheeks flushed candyfloss pink. Another was heavily made-up like an old-time showgirl, all long lashes and lips. The third was patched with pockmarks the colour of red cabbage, yellow eyes glaring from its shrunken head.

The ride careered faster and faster and sent me reeling into a carriage pulled by three horses. My head was pinned to the back of the seat from the force of the spinning. I stared up at the stars and planets painted on the underside of the canopy. Everything became a whirl of ruby and gold, silver and blue, then red and white. I closed my eyes, surrendering myself to the flow as the ride ran its course. It stuttered to a standstill, and the music faltered and wheezed to nothing. Finally, the shutters snapped back over the lanterns. I staggered from the carriage, but couldn't see where the edge of the platform was. It was as if the carousel had merged with the ground.

When the music eventually stopped ringing in my ears, I realised another set of sounds had replaced it. Whistles and chirps, and the rush of water, and then the hammer of hooves. I turned cold with sweat. I'd hated being anywhere near horses since the time one went crazy and nearly got Granny killed. We were on holiday in Germany at the time, somewhere near the border with France, and the horse she was riding bolted off the path into the traffic. A lorry had to swerve right across the road to avoid her. It was so close. *So* close – and so were these. They were just a few metres away. Two out-of-control horses – one black, the other white – were pounding towards me.

* * *

'Lolly!' called a little girl, stabbing a finger into the air. 'Listen! Music.' She climbed further up the branch she was perched on. 'It's *the* music. From the carousel.'

'Stop making things up. It can't be.'

'There. Listen!'

Lola froze. Her sister was right.

'Why is it playing now, Lolly? It's not time, is it? There haven't been enough moons or suns since the last time. This is the first day, isn't it?'

Lola leapt down from the tree.

'Where are you going?'

'To see what's happening.'

'You can't. You mustn't. Wait! Don't leave me.' Coco went after her sister. 'We're not supposed to do this, Lolly. We're not supposed to leave. We shouldn't have come as far as this.'

'We're not leaving, and we can't go any further. It's not *possible* to go further. We're just checking. *I'm* just checking. You can stay here if you like.'

'I want to come with you.'

'Only if you're quiet, and stay close.'

They went as far as they could, to the edge of the mist, and sat on the mossy ground watching the swirling lights, bodies quivering like hummingbirds.

'What can you see, Lolly? Are the others there? Have they left us out? Why would they do that?'

'Shh!' Lola stood up as the music machine wound down.

'What is it? What are you looking at?'

'Nothing.' Lola pulled Coco close. She'd seen a girl on the

carousel, which shouldn't be possible, because this wasn't the time, this wasn't what happened. She stroked her sister's hair. Both girls put their hands to their ears as two horses charged through the mist towards them. The black mare stopped. It reared up, snorting, and stampeded off. The white horse emerged with the girl draped across the saddle in front of the hooded rider. All at once, it became light as day. Lola grabbed her sister and lurched from the beast's path. She raised her head and watched as the rider dropped the girl to the ground and rode off.

Chapter Seven

I'd fallen hard and there were bits of bracken stuck in the blood on my knees. I picked them out, then picked myself up. There was no sign of the horses or their riders. They'd left as quickly as they'd come, before I could ask where I was, or why they'd picked me up. But at least there was light now. At least I could see. I was in a kind of forest, but not like one I'd ever seen before. The tree trunks were completely encased in leaves, with bare branches reaching out through them like grabbing hands. And there were plants bigger than houses, with spiky green fronds and orange tips fanned out like peacock feathers.

I looked back to where I thought I'd come from. I couldn't see the carousel. There was no path or anything to suggest I should go this way or that way, or any way at all. I heard a shuffling sound. I spun round.

'Who's there?' I heard giggling. 'Is someone there?'

'We're here, silly!' A scrawny, fair-haired child came from behind a tree. 'We found you. We were playing hide and seek to find you, and we won! We found you! I'm Coco and this is my sister Lola. I call her Lolly, and when we sing we're called "Miss Lola Lemona and Coco Coo". Shall we sing for her, Lolly?'

A second girl appeared at her side. She was taller and had darker hair, but she had the same piercing grey-blue eyes and was just as bony as the little one. They both wore feathery dresses that hung loosely from their fragile frames; one gold, the other redcurrant. I shrank back, but it wasn't just their mad-crazy staring eyes and outfits that disturbed me. It was their skin. Their faces were wrinkly and veiny. Their necks looked like plucked chicken skin. And their *teeth*. Their teeth were little black stumps, like bits of broken coal. They were like little-girl grannies, and they both just stood there, looking me up and down with their stabbing eyes, saying nothing, scrutinising me.

It was only then I realised I was wearing a thin nightdress. I'd never seen it before and definitely didn't remember putting it on, but it had a small pocket at the front, so I put Granny's doll in it to keep her safe, and folded my arms to hide myself.

'No. No singing,' said the older girl, pushing her sister behind her. 'Who are you?' she asked. 'What are you doing here?'

'I . . . I don't know. I think I'm . . . I might be lost. Which way is Highfield?'

'You really are lost. There isn't anything called that here. There's just us.'

'Quiet, Coco. Why haven't we seen you before? Where's Mother Matushka been keeping you?'

'Who?' I took a step back. Her eyes were burning into me.

'You must know Mother.' Coco frowned. 'You have to

58

know Mother. She's everything. She's *more* than everything.'

I didn't know what was worse, randomly finding myself in a graveyard, or being interrogated by these terrifying girls. I felt trapped. 'Look, I don't know who you're talking about or how I ended up here. Can't you just tell me how to get back to a road? There must be someone who can help.' My voice broke. I breathed deep to try to calm myself down. 'Do you have a phone? Where are your mum and dad?'

'Our mother and father aren't here, silly.'

'But you just asked me about your mother.'

'She's not just *our* mother, silly. She's everyone's mother. She's Mother Matushka. You talk funny. Can I touch you?' Coco prodded my arm. Her fingers were icy cold and made me shiver, but she reacted with more than a shiver. She sprang away from me like I'd given her an electric shock. 'She feels funny, Lolly. And there's blood on her. Look, *blood*!'

She looked horrified. My knees did look pretty rank from the fall but there wasn't that much blood. But then I noticed she wasn't just staring at my knees. She was staring at my head too. I touched where it hurt. My hand came away sticky.

'How can she be *bleeding*? She's like a real girl, isn't she, Lolly? She's not like a shadow.'

'Of course I'm real. What do you mean?'

Lola grabbed my wrist with her scaly hands. She clenched me so hard I thought my bones would snap. She was far stronger than she looked.

'Get off me!' I had to use all my strength to pull away from her. I darted off, vaguely in the direction I'd come from, but I'd only gone a few steps when I felt myself sinking. Within seconds the salty mud was up to my waist, and gluey plant fronds were swirling up around my neck.

'Help me!' I screamed. 'I'm drowning.'

The swamp was closing in around me, sucking at my ribs and shoulders. I could hardly breathe. I was certain that this was it; I was going to be pulled under and die. I went to raise my arms, to keep myself up, but they were bound to my sides by the suffocating sludge. I could feel hot mud bubbling into my face. I didn't know if it was preparing to suck me under or spit me out, and the more I struggled, the deeper I sank. I had to calm down or I'd be gone. But if I did nothing, I'd be gone too. I had to do *something*, and fast.

'Find something for me to grab onto,' I called. 'Just make it stop!'

I concentrated all my strength into keeping my head up, then twisted my hips and tried to shake my right leg loose without moving too erratically.

Come on, come on. I felt something shift.

'It's all right now,' Coco giggled. 'You can stop wiggling. You can get out. Look!'

Keeping my head tilted back, I lowered my eyes. Coco was right. The mud had thinned out and I could move freely. I was still up to my hips in murky water, but I could move. I freed my arms and burst out crying and laughing all at the same time, hysterical with relief as I waded back to the edge of the marsh. I wasn't at all religious, but at that moment, I wanted to thank someone up there for saving me. I felt like I'd experienced a miracle.

When I reached the bank, Lola was staring at me like I

had three heads. 'What is it?' I asked. 'I could have drowned, you know. It was up to my neck.'

'You made the marsh go,' said Lola.

The way she said it really creeped me out. It was like she thought I had some weird powers, or had performed some kind of black magic to make it happen, or something. It had *felt* magical, but that was just my massive relief that I hadn't drowned. It's amazing what keeping calm and focused can do. Or maybe I was just lucky. But I definitely didn't do anything to *make* it go.

'You have to see Mother. You really do.' Lola grabbed hold of me again. I struggled against her. I was freaked out. The marsh, these girls – the way they looked, the way they spoke; it wasn't normal. It was like they, and this place, existed outside the normal world. I turned back to where we'd come from, but I couldn't see more than a few paces ahead. A strange mist had suddenly descended, and it was swirling towards us.

Crap. I couldn't see my way back to the carousel or graveyard now. In a split second, I wondered about breaking free from Lola and trying to find my way out, but the way the mist was now closing in, licking its vaporous limbs against me like a living thing, I decided I'd be better off going with them. This Mother person might be able to help me get out of this freaky place.

We went deeper into the forest, faster and faster, with the mist chasing at our heels. We swerved sharply to the right and stopped on the edge of a crater. There were clouds beneath us, forming a kind of cocoon over it. I stepped back from the edge, my head spinning and hands clammy from being up so high. It was like looking down through the sky. Then I felt a rumbling and a droning vibration rising through my feet, like the earth was throbbing, and through the mist I could see a settlement in the valley below. There was an enormous red-and-white Big Top at its centre, ringed by trees.

'Is this a circus? You're from a circus?'

'It's not just a circus, silly,' said Coco. 'We're a secret. We're the Circus of the Unseen.'

'What do you mean?'

'Well, have *you* seen it before?'

I supposed Lola had a point. I hadn't seen it before, but then, why would I have? I didn't know where I was. I might have been a few miles from home, or a million. She took hold of me again and we swooped into the valley. The bank was steep, almost vertical, and we plunged down so fast it felt like we were actually flying and I'd left my stomach on the edge. The momentum was so strong I carried on hurtling forwards, even after we'd reached the bottom.

When I eventually stopped and caught my breath, I heard music again, but this sounded like real musicians were playing it. I couldn't see them clearly through the trees, but I could see movement, and could hear violins being bowed, cellos being stroked, drums being struck. The noise made me feel queasy. All the jerky strings, and honking horns and a clanking piano that sounded like someone was dancing up and down on the keys. It sounded like a wonky-wheeled cart, and every time the music skipped a beat it was like the cart had hit a rock and was about to overturn. But there was something keeping it upright. Through the madness of it all, beyond the chaos, a calm drone underpinned everything. And then I saw the source of the drone. There was a girl sitting alone, away from the trees, away from the others. She was dressed in a kind of traditional folk costume, working the bellows of her accordion as if it was part of her, not just an attachment strapped to her chest. She couldn't have been more than five, but her music was . . . I don't know, it sounded wise. She sounded older than her years. I closed my eyes and found myself swaying in time with the music.

The spell was broken by a jab in my ribs.

'Through here, and stay behind me.'

I followed Lola through an avenue of trees and we came to another sweet-smelling grove like the one I'd found after the graveyard, except this had the Big Top at its centre rather than a carousel – and it really was enormous, bigger than any other circus I'd been to, bigger than any stadium. It was like an upscaled version of the old-fashioned fair Daisy and I had been to years ago, the one we'd had our photo taken at. But this wasn't exactly like that. There were no lorries here spoiling the old-time atmosphere. This was like *being* in the old time. No behind-the-scenes grime, no chug of generators belching out dirty smoke. No safety nets, backstage workers or laser light shows ruining the out-of-this-world illusion. There were flaming torches and flickering lanterns. There were ropes and wires and giant seesaws and springboards. There were girls twirling on dancing horses, divers in stripy swimsuits plunging from high boards into tanks of bubbling water. Everyone was wearing some kind of elaborate costume, robes from the ancient world, beautiful black-and-red African masks, carnival headdresses, sweet-wrapper-bright kimonos. It was like people from all places and all times had gathered here.

'Scarlie! Look what we found, Scarlie. A surprise!'

Coco waved madly at a woman strapped to a Wheel of Death contraption. It was spinning round at a crazy speed, making her red hair spray out like flames. Coco ran to a basket near the wheel and picked up a knife. 'Ready?' Coco called. The woman grinned and Coco hurled the knife at her. It skimmed her hand, stabbed into the board between her thumb and index finger. Then she did it again and again, and I swear every single knife Coco launched touched some part of the woman's body. I couldn't bear to watch. I looked away.

'Should she be doing this?' I asked Lola. Then, just as I finished speaking, Coco let out an ear-piercing shriek. There was a blade planted deep in the woman's neck, right down to the handle. *Jesus.* I needed to spew. Lola ran to the wheel and spun it round so the woman's feet were at the bottom. Then she yanked out the knife and unstrapped her. I couldn't believe it when she stepped down and took a bow as if nothing had happened. I couldn't see how this was an illusion. This looked like an actual death-defying feat. I mean, this really should have killed her.

'Scarlet's special, isn't she?' Coco smiled. 'We're all special here.'

'So what's this surprise then, honey?' The woman who should have been dead swaggered towards me in swishing skirts and a pair of lace-up boots that were as tight as a second skin. She stopped a metre or so away, one hand on her pinched-in waist, looking like she'd slipped off the pages of a comic book, or an old pin-up poster advert for a once-fashionable brand of cola.

'We found a new girl, Scarlie! I heard the music and then we found her.'

'Thought no one had stayed last time round.' The woman flicked her hair to the side. 'Scarlet Starlet,' she said, holding out a hand. I noticed a tear in the thumb of her glove. The knives must have been real, sharp enough to cut through leather. 'And who are you?' she asked. 'Where did you come from back there? Pretty little thing, aren't you? What's your name, girl?'

'Rosie,' I said, staring at her neck. The only mark I could see was a tattoo near her collarbone, an anchor with a mermaid coiled around its base, and the words 'Captain Jack Forever' beneath it. No hole, and not even a cut or a graze where I'd definitely seen the knife go in. Just that tattoo on her perfectly smooth skin. 'That looked so real. How did you do it?'

'A showgirl *never* reveals her secrets.' She smiled. 'So, where did you find her, Lola?'

'She was out near the edge. We heard the music and wondered why it was playing. So we went to the edge and found her there. I thought we should come straight here to find Mother.'

A look of horror spread over Scarlet's face. 'No. That's not right. It's not possible. The carousel was playing? Just now?'

'She said she came on the carousel, but she was on her own, and she doesn't know who Mother is. She says she doesn't know anything.' Lola scanned the area around the Big Top. 'Where is Mother?'

'In the forest with Fabian. There's something going on with the animals.' Scarlet glanced at me as she spoke. 'Don't know what exactly,' she went on, 'but he asked her to give him a hand.'

'I'll take her to the forest, then,' said Lola. It was like I wasn't there.

Scarlet took hold of Lola's shoulders and leaned in really close so their noses were almost touching. 'The thing is, Lola, if you take her, Mother will know you went too far, and she might be inclined to think you were trying to leave, and you know what would happen then, don't you? You don't want to end up like Freddie, do you?'

Lola looked at her feet and shook her head. 'I'm nothing like him,' she murmured. 'We weren't trying to leave. We really weren't. Don't tell Mother we were, will you?' Her voice was loud and pleading now. 'Because we weren't. We'd never do that. *Never.*'

'That's not what it looks like. Let me handle this. She can wait at my place. Mother will come for her. She'll know something's not right. Besides, it's nearly time for sundown. Mother will be back for that, won't she?'

'I'll go. Let me find her,' I said. I couldn't stand it any longer, the way they were all treating me like *I* was the freak.

'I mean, if she's the only one who can help me, I'll just find her myself. Or do you have a phone? I just need to know how to get home, that's all. Please.' My voice cracked.

'I don't know what's going on, but getting worked up won't help anyone. Calm down, kid. You're coming home with me, for now. I'll take care of you until Mother comes.'

Seeing as that was the closest thing I'd had to an offer of help since I'd got here, I went with her. What else could I do?

Chapter Eight

Scarlet's home was a curvy-roofed wagon, set back from a river, beneath a cluster of willow trees. From the outside it looked like a fortuneteller's den. Her name was swirled across the side, curled around a life-size painting of her standing astride a horse. I guessed being able to survive a Wheel of Death wasn't her only circus skill. And then I saw the horse, just to the side of the wagon. It was a shiny, russet creature, really elegant and docile-looking, but still, I kept my distance from it.

Scarlet ushered me up the steps and through the door. Inside, it reminded me of an old theatre that had seen better days. Velvet drapes sagged from the ceiling and one wall was entirely covered with mismatched mirrors. She hitched up her skirts and settled in the middle of the room on a heap of cushions.

'We just need to sit tight until Mother comes,' she said. 'Shouldn't be long.'

So we sat in silence, her watching my every move. Eventually, I suggested again that I could go and find this Mother woman myself, but Scarlet said it would be dark soon and I'd have no chance of finding anything, so I really should stay here. I'd lost all sense of time. It was nighttime when I was in the graveyard, and she was talking about it getting dark again. Was this already my second night away from home? I had no idea, and then I started to panic about what Mum and Dad were thinking, and how I was going to get back to them. We both jumped when we heard someone coming up the steps.

'See, what did I tell you? That'll be Mother Matushka. She'll know what to do, she'll know why it's happened.' I think both our hearts sank when we saw it was Lola. 'Did you speak to Mother?' Scarlet asked. 'What does she want me to do? Is she on her way over?'

'I haven't seen her. Maybe she's still with Fabian. But I fetched some of the soup for the girl.'

'What the hell's keeping her? And sundown is late, isn't it? But I reckon the soup is a good idea, thank you, Lola. Here you go, girl.' Scarlet handed me the bowl. 'One helping of this will fill you for all eternity. Matushka's broth is good for the body, but even better for the soul. It's what all new arrivals have. Now eat it all up while I have a word with Lola.'

The dollops of brown sludge didn't look at all appetising, and there were bones bobbing beneath the surface, but it smelled really good and I realised how hungry I was. I hadn't eaten a thing since I'd made breakfast for Mum and me and that was . . . I don't know. It was ages ago. I tried a drop. It tasted far better than it looked, and even better than it smelled. By the time Scarlet came back, I'd wolfed it all down, except for the greasy bones. She came right up to me and pushed back the hair from my forehead. Her hands were trembling.

'It *is* blood!' she gasped. And, actually, it wasn't just her hands that were trembling; her whole body was, and her voice. 'Lola was right. You shouldn't be here, girl. You really shouldn't.' She wiped her fingers on her skirts, like she thought I might have something contagious.

'I know,' I said, under my breath. 'I feel exactly the same.'

'And what did you do to the marsh? How did you do it?'

I didn't understand why they kept going on about the marsh. I mean, almost drowning was obviously one of the worst things I'd ever experienced, but it wasn't like I'd actually done anything. 'You know what?' I said. 'I just tried not to drown. I tried really damn hard not to drown, and I didn't. I was lucky. There's no mystery to it. What about you and the knife? It was right in your neck. How did you do that?'

Scarlet charged to the door. She clearly wasn't going to reveal any of her secrets. And then I wondered if that's what they were thinking about me and the marsh – that it was a weird circus trick they'd never seen before.

'Where the hell is Mother?' She scanned the area outside the wagon, then turned back to me. 'You should get cleaned up before she gets here. I'll draw a bath.'

After making several trips to and from the river with a bucket, Scarlet pulled back a screen to reveal a tub full of steaming water. I don't know how she'd heated it, unless the river was actually a hot spring. Maybe I shouldn't have been thinking about how nice it would be to lie down and get everything out of my head for a few minutes. Maybe I should have just made a run for it, but the truth was, I felt completely exhausted and had a pounding headache and a bath seemed like a good idea.

'Jump in,' she said. 'Jump in and scrub off all that blood and marsh-mud.'

I pulled the screen across, peeled off the dirty nightdress and plunged into the water. After lying there a few minutes, letting the warm water do its work, I began to relax and my headache eased.

'How long do you stay in each place you visit?' I asked, wondering what it would be like to travel around all the time, and not have a permanent home. 'Were you all born into it?'

'We don't move, girl. People come to us, and no one is born here. That's not how it works.' She stuck her head round the screen. 'So you really don't know *anything* about this place? What exactly happened before the girls found you?'

In the time it took me to tell her the exact same thing I'd told the sisters, all the good the bath had done was undone and I was itching with panic again. 'Why do I have to wait for this Mother person? Why can't I just leave?'

'There's not exactly a road out, same way there's not exactly a road in.' She handed me a towel and clean nightdress. 'And I can't have you wandering around out there. Need to keep an eye on you, don't I? Dry yourself and get some rest. Up you go. Bed. Sleep. I'll wake you when Mother comes.'

I was too tired to argue so I climbed the ladder up to the bed, holding my doll. It was basically a mattress and heap of cushions on top of what looked like a cupboard, but it was really cosy, especially when Scarlet tucked me in. I hadn't been tucked in for years.

'What a darling charm,' she said. 'Real rubies?'

I touched my neck. 'It was my grandmother's. She died.' It still hurt to say it aloud. It still made the tears swell and my throat close up, and I still wasn't good at hiding it.

'I don't know what the hell you're doing here, but you're still just a child, aren't you? You are, aren't you?' she repeated, like she was trying to convince herself that's all I was. 'Don't cry, girl There's plenty who don't make it to grandmahood, and there's plenty of girls who never know their grandmas. If I were you, I'd think of how lucky she was to have become one, and how lucky I was to have met her. No point ruining your life over death, is there? That's a lesson best learned early. Now rest. Things always seem better when you wake up. Well, they *usually* do. Now close your eyes.'

The way Scarlet was babbling and staring at the cut on my head made it clear she wasn't sure that things really would be better when I woke, but I was too shattered to do anything else right then. My body curled itself up and I closed my eyes.

Chapter Nine

Mother Matushka was old, a sallow bag of bones. She'd seen everything with those sharp eyes, done everything with those sinewy hands. You didn't get to her age without knowing a thing or two. *Older than the earth, and stronger than it too*, she affirmed to herself as she made her way back through the forest to the Big Top. She could see the torches around it now, flickering wildly in the airstreams her performers were making. They'd be wondering where she was. She was already late drawing down the light and releasing them to their rest. The animals had settled, eventually, but would they stay calm? And why had it taken two of them? That wasn't usually the case. Had the Fabulous Fabianski lost a little of his fabulousness? Or was it something else? For the first time in her existence Mother Matushka did not have the answer.

She came to the edge of the valley and looked out over the Big Top, its red-and-white skin stretched tight over the bones of its frame. She raised her arms – scrawny wings with flaps of skin in place of feathers – and snapped her fingers. One by one, the torches extinguished and the performers stopped what they were doing and lay down for the night.

Next, she performed the drawing down of light. She pulled her arms to her sides, slow and calm, and the Circus of the Unseen became as unseen to those inside as it was to those outside.

The joints of Matushka's skinny legs grated as she made her way home, but she moved as nimbly as a girl. She came to her cottage and sparked up flames on her fence-posts. She called for her wolves, and she sent them out to guard the seals around her circus. Once again, she raised her arms to the sky. Then she lowered them, and a stream of birds slipped from the sleeves of her cloak. Their black feathers shimmered purple and green as they crashed into each other, spiralling and lurching in all directions. Matushka outlined a path in the sky with a finger, the same path, over and over again, until the birds followed her invisible trail. They looped around the cottage, then she slowed them, and she drew them down.

They followed her inside, and while they settled in the rafters, cooing and scratching and fluffing their feathers, Mother Matushka went to her hearth to seal all around it. She scattered soil, and then salt, and pressed down hard, to close any gaps, to keep things contained, for that's what she did, for that's how it must be.

Then she lay down by the fire to rest, but she tossed and turned. She flailed and thrashed. She itched with the sense that something wasn't right. She got up and squinted into the pot hanging over the hearth, and she saw that some of her soup was missing. It was always on the boil here, simmering over the fire, ready to nourish those newcomers who would stay and make this their home. She was no fool. It was always replenished to the same amount, maintained to the same volume, so it was obvious some had gone. Only a bowlful, but theft was theft and all the worse because there was no reason to steal it. Everyone was fed all they needed when they first came into her charge. No one *needed* more. And what child would take from their mother? While Matushka had birthed no children of her own, she was mother to many. She was mother to everyone here. All their lives revolved around her, all paths led to her cottage, all water came from her lake and her river, and she knew everything there was to know. Or so she'd thought. She did not know about the animals, and now the missing soup. For the second time in her existence Mother Matushka did not have an answer. She scattered more salt and earth and tried, again, to rest.

Chapter Ten

I was curled up in Scarlet's snuggly bed, but I just couldn't settle. The wagon was itchy-hot, and my brain was throbbing with worry about how I'd get home, and what Mum and Dad must be thinking. I sort of wished I had someone to talk to, but Scarlet was sound asleep. I could see her lying among the cushions, completely still and silent. I turned to face the wall and closed my eyes again.

Throughout the night, as I slipped in and out of sleep, I was haunted by the same dream, over and over, though it felt more real than any dream. I could see Mum and Dad standing over me with Daisy tucked between them. They were all blurry and the room was spinning. Its white walls were fuzzy, and the stomach-churning stench of bleach burned my nostrils. I went to sit up, but my body was numb. I couldn't move, but I still felt like I was falling, and I could feel Granny's doll in my hand. That was all I could feel.

'What will we do? What are we supposed to do?' Mum asked in this tiny voice.

What's wrong, Mum? I asked. *Where am I?*

But Mum didn't answer.

Daisy stepped forward. 'How could Granny have done it?' she asked, her voice all choked and spluttery. 'How could she?'

What is it, Daisy? What's wrong?

'If it hadn't been for what Granny did, this wouldn't have happened to Rosie, would it? She wouldn't be lying here like this.'

WHAT WOULDN'T HAVE HAPPENED, DAISY? WHY CAN'T YOU HEAR ME?

'Don't say that, Daisy. Don't say it.' Dad took hold of her and she started screaming and sobbing.

'Stop it. Just stop it!' Mum was frantic too. 'Blame me, not Granny. Blame me. I knew about them. I knew she'd been married before.'

WHY DIDN'T YOU TELL US, MUM? WHY DIDN'T YOU SAY?

Mum stroked my hair.

'I love you, darling. I'm sorry, I'm so sorry.'

She broke down on Dad's shoulder, and Daisy started shaking like crazy, and a pale green curtain closed around us, and I screamed at the top of my lungs.

WHY CAN'T YOU HEAR ME? WHAT'S WRONG WITH YOU?

I was woken by something tickling my nose. There were fronds reaching through the open roof hatch, filling the air with the smell of leaves and sickly-sweet flowers. I sat bolt upright. I wasn't dreaming any more. I was awake, and still in the wagon in this weird place.

'Sleep well?' asked Scarlet. She was standing right next to the bed. She must have been watching, waiting for me to wake up. Why hadn't she just woken me? She *should* have woken me. I hadn't meant to stay the whole night.

'The sun coming up doesn't really make bad things go away, does it?' I said, swinging my legs over the bed. 'I mean, it's definitely not true that things always seem better in the morning. I need to go. I have to get out of here.'

'Don't get worked up, girl. We're going to get you dressed up real nice and then we'll go to Mother. I was certain she was going to come last night, but you don't always get what you want, do you?'

Scarlet opened the cupboard under the bed. It was actually a wardrobe, stuffed with dozens of dresses and costumes. I could see at least five feather boas. 'I'm sure we can find something for you here. It's like a dressing-up box of the whole world, don't you think?' She rooted through the clothes, telling me the story of every outfit she pulled out. 'This beauty takes me back,' she said, swirling around with an emerald evening gown. It was split to the thigh and flicked out at the bottom like a mermaid's tail. 'Made its debut at the Hollywood premiere of *The Wrong Kind of Girl*. You know, the one where Marilyn plays a two-bit singer stuck in a blizzard at a bus stop with a rodeo star?'

'Haven't seen it,' I huffed. I couldn't help it. I'm sure they all had an interesting story, but the way she was going on about each and every dress was starting to drive me crazy. 'Is this going to take much longer?'

'I was a performer back then too,' she went on, ignoring

me. 'I worked the trapeze until my pregnant belly got too big for me to fly. I did a bit of acting, too, which is how I got invited to the premiere.'

'But that would have been decades ago,' I said, wondering why she was lying, and annoyed she thought I was that gullible. 'You're not old enough.'

'Maybe I am, and maybe I'm not. You'd be surprised, girl. You'd be surprised what a layer or two of make-up and a damn good outfit can do. I know all the tricks of the trade. I can show you some if you like. You'd look good with some colour in your cheeks.'

'Look, don't worry about me.' She was definitely trying to stall leaving. 'I'll wear anything. I'm not fussy. Then I'll get out of your way. I'm sure you have other things to do, like get ready for the performance.'

'And *you* don't need to worry about *that*. You're not keeping me from anything – there's no performance today. Doesn't work like that. We're not any old circus, you know.'

'Let me guess. This is the Greatest Show on Earth, right?'

'Uh-uh.' She shook her head. 'We're the Greatest Show *Beyond* Earth, honey, and make no mistake.'

'So if there's not a show today, why are you all dressed up?' Her glamorous riding outfit (tight white jodhpurs, a black jacket with tails and a shiny top hat) was hardly something you'd wear to muck out the stables.

'I don't call it dressing up, girl. I call it *dressing*. I mean, why save things for best? I didn't do that before I came here, and there's definitely no point doing it here.'

Scarlet saying that made me think of Granny. She never

saw any point saving things for some imaginary special day in the future either, but sensing Scarlet was about to go off in another direction that would delay us even more, I took the liberty of picking out something for myself. 'How about this?' It was a red-and-white polka-dot dress, one of the few not made from sheer silk or covered in sequins or feathers, and it had pockets at the front, like an apron, perfect for keeping the doll in.

'Reckon it'll look pretty good on you, reckon it'll fit like a gl—' Scarlet froze. 'Did you hear something?' She gripped my arm and peered out of the window. 'It's Fabian.' She looked relieved. 'Maybe Mother's with him. Get yourself ready while I check.' She closed the door behind her.

I pulled on the dress and went to the wall of mirrors. I have to admit it did look pretty good, and I felt good in it too. The bodice part was tight, and I wasn't used to wearing halter necks and having bare shoulders, but it wasn't so over-the-top revealing that I felt massively self-conscious. I mean, I could cope with it, so I went outside.

Scarlet smiled when she saw me. 'You look sensational, girl. Bet your daddy adores you. What did I tell you, Fab? I told you she was a darling. You can see why I couldn't leave her out there on her own, can't you? You can understand it, right? You can't blame me for taking her in. Rosie, meet the Fabulous Fabianski. Fabian to his friends. And that's his daughter, Accordienka.'

I recognised the girl. She was the accordionist, a delicate-looking thing with striking features. She had these big, brown eyes and a wide, cat-like face, with sharp cheekbones. The

Fabulous Fabianski was pretty striking too. He was tall and handsome, despite his odd clothes. He was dressed like an old-fashioned huntsman, in a loose white shirt rolled up at the sleeves and puffy trousers tucked into his boots. I couldn't help but notice how muscly and tanned his forearms were. I guess he spent a lot of time working outside. He stepped towards me and held my gaze for what felt like an age.

'A beautiful name,' he said, staring right into me. I couldn't quite place his accent. He voice was deep and steady, with a gentle lilt. 'Little Rose.'

'What did I tell you?' Scarlet smiled.

Fabian scratched his stubble and turned to her, now looking more agitated than curious. 'What did Matushka have to say about this? Why did this girl arrive at the wrong time? Is she supposed to stay, or should she have left?'

My heart sank. I guess I'd been hoping he'd talk some sense, like a normal person who'd know what to do to make this weirdness end. But, at the same time, I found myself thinking that I could listen to Fabian all day. He had a perfect storytelling voice. It sounded like . . . like unsweetened honey, or something; smooth and sharp at the same time. I reckoned he'd never actually been to England, but the archaic way he phrased things was really charming.

'What did Mother say?' he repeated, actually sounding angry now, and I mentally slapped myself for daydreaming.

'Well, that's the thing . . .' Scarlet bit her lower lip.

'You mean Mother doesn't know? You haven't told her? What were you thinking, Scarlet?'

'Don't raise your voice at me, Fab. I did what I thought

was best. I thought Mother would have known about her and come last night. But she didn't, and I couldn't just kick her out, could I? So I suggested she rest until Mother came. Then she fell asleep and now it's morning.' Scarlet looked at the sky. 'Though it hardly looks like it. What's up with the sun? Why is it so dim?'

I'd never seen the sun so pale either. It was almost silver. A faint, lunar-looking disc, low down in the sky. Eerie and beautiful – but I just wished they'd get on with doing something to help me.

'And the sun setting was late last night too, wasn't it?' Scarlet glanced at me. 'But you can't blame me for letting her spend the night here, can you? I really thought Mother would come.'

'Perhaps she didn't because of these irregularities with the light, and the animals,' Fabian suggested. 'I understand why you did what you did, but you need to see her immediately, Scarlet. This newcomer is not your doll.'

I was about to tell him that I definitely wasn't anyone's doll and just needed directions, when Accordienka bounded towards us and waggled something in her father's face. She dropped whatever it was. As I went to pick it up, she snatched it away and hid behind his legs.

'She doesn't mean to be rude,' Fabian explained. 'But she's very precious about her little doll. Her mother gave it to her, you see.'

'No worries.' I shrugged, wondering if the mother was still around, because it seemed to me that there might be something between Fabian and Scarlet. They'd make a stunning couple.

'You never let her out of your sight, do you, my darling?

You look after each other, don't you?'

I shivered. A full-body shudder that started as an icy tingle in the base of my neck and ran all the way through to my toes. I touched my doll, and thought of what Granny had said about it looking after me, and I thought of the story she'd mentioned, the one about Vasilisa. I'd have to read it as soon as I got back, as soon as Mum had calmed down.

'So, we shall go to Mother, yes?' Fabian rubbed his hands together. 'We shall go and explain, all of us together.'

'Thank you, Fabian. I'd prefer not to go alone.' Scarlet planted a kiss on his cheek. 'Can always depend on you to stay calm. Never get in a flap, do you? Just give me five seconds and we'll go.' She dashed back up the steps to the wagon.

While Scarlet was faffing around inside and Fabian and Accordienka went to see her horse, I walked a little way along the path that followed the river. The air was hot and heavy, and the trees were weighed down with exotic flowers that looked like fruit. I looked over my shoulder. I couldn't see them, so I carried on wandering towards a crossroads that forked off in three directions. While I was trying to decide which way to go, a pair of fluffy puppies, maybe huskies, bounded up to me. Their tails were waggling like crazy and they had incredibly intense blue eyes.

'Hello there!' I ruffled their heads and they both clamped their teeth into my dress. There were vicious snarls, and flashes of teeth and icy-blue eyes. 'Get off!' I shouted. 'Stop it!' They were trying to drag me in the direction they had come from. 'It's all right, I'm coming. I'm coming with you.'

I could see a cottage at the end of the path. It looked more

86

like a proper house than anything else I'd seen here. Someone had to live in it. Someone there had to be able to help. As soon as I stopped struggling, the dogs released me and I walked towards the cottage with them jostling at my legs.

Up close, I could see it was far from normal. The building was perched about a metre off the ground on stilts, all squat and plump, like a nesting hen, and there was a thin stick jutting through the roof. A skull capped each of the fence posts, and the windows and roof were framed with beaks and bird skulls. I'd have been less surprised if it had been decorated with candy and gingerbread. The only things that looked relatively normal were the rose plants around the porch area, except they were blue. I never knew you could get blue ones.

I walked to the door through a scattering of silky petals. It had a complicated lock that looked like an iron jaw, with jagged teeth protecting the keyhole. The dogs jumped up and scratched at the door. The jaw snapped, the door opened. I peeped inside.

It was dark, lit only by the glow from the fire. A huge spinning wheel filled most of the space, and there was hardly any furniture – just a table, a couple of stools and a heap of rags in front of the fire. The only other things I noticed were a steaming pot on the fire and a shelf overhead, hanging from the ceiling. As I looked up at it, I lost my balance and tripped on the bundle of rags.

The bundle juddered. It was hairy and bony and had sharp little teeth.

Chapter Eleven

The bundle was a person, an ancient-looking woman glaring at me through glassy, gold eyes, like an eagle's. Tight coils of silver and brown hair wound round and round her head, and the skin on her face was like smoked bacon rind, yellowed and slack over her bones. She waggled the tails of her cloak, furiously. I wasn't sure what she meant, but I wondered if she wanted help getting out of it, so I lifted it from her shoulders. It was an incredibly heavy patchwork of different animal parts. Skin, fur, wool, and claws too, I noticed, as something scratched my arm. Freed from its mass, I saw that her shoulder blades jutted through her smock like stunted wings. She took the cloak from me as if it weighed nothing, and laid it in front of the fire.

'You boys took longer than I thought.' She was talking to the dogs. She turned to me and stared hard with her animal eyes. 'So *you* are the cause of the disruption,' she rasped. Her voice was crackly as leaves. 'What do you want with this world?'

This had to be Mother Matushka. I just knew it and, in an instant, I felt more trapped than ever. The person everyone said would be able to help me was asking the same questions as everyone else. I was going round in circles.

'Nothing. I don't want anything here,' I said. 'I'm lost, and they said you'd know what to do. You are Mother Matushka, aren't you? I just want to go home.'

'Yes,' she said, drawing the word out with a hiss. 'Yes, I am Mother Matushka, and sometimes I am *Madam* Matushka, Mistress of the Greatest Show Beyond Earth, of this Circus of the Unseen. And you say you "just" want to go home?' She smiled. A nasty, knowing smile that made my insides scrunch. 'You are not the first to have wanted that, but you *are* the first to have broken my seal to be here.'

I went to speak, to tell her I'd done nothing, I'd broken nothing – not intentionally anyway – but she lunged towards me. I gasped and froze, but all she did was press a finger to my mouth to silence me. Her touch was gentle, her skin surprisingly soft, but I stayed statue-still, scared of what she'd do next. She looked so frail and small – she only came up to my shoulders – but the way she'd taken that heavy cloak from me showed how strong she was. The thing that scared me the most, though, was having no idea what she was thinking. Now I knew why Scarlet had been putting off coming here.

'At present, there is much darkness about this situation,' she went on. 'And it is not good to be in darkness. How can the sun have slipped? How can that be?'

I followed her outside. She walked halfway down the path and turned back to face the cottage. Then she held out her arms and clenched both fists, almost like she was gripping an invisible wheel with her claw-like hands. She pushed down, slow and taut, grunting from the effort. And I swear as her arms turned that invisible wheel clockwise, I saw the sun begin to rise. I swear it looked like she was making the sun move higher. It was now above the cottage. I couldn't believe what I'd seen. It had to be an illusion, a circus trick. Maybe the view behind the cottage wasn't real. Maybe it was like a stage set, a backdrop. Maybe what I thought was the sun was actually fake, just a circle lit up from behind a screen, and someone was there watching us, moving the light up in line with Mother Matushka's hands. I ran towards the trees behind the cottage, and towards the sun, but I didn't crash into a painted background, and there wasn't a screen, or a light or a technician or anything like that. It seemed as real as anything.

'How did you do that?' I asked. 'What's the trick?'

'Trick? There is no trick.' She looked offended. 'And I did it with difficulty, that's how I did it, which is not normally the case, and I believe that is your fault, like the animals are your fault.'

'I don't know anything about the animals. Why do you think they have anything to do with me?'

'I shall ask the questions. Inside,' she ordered, but hesitated in the doorway. She picked up a rose petal and brought it to her nose. 'Why have these dropped? Why have they wilted? Is this your doing too?' she asked. I had no answer. She shepherded me to a stool. 'Sit. There is much to discuss, so many things to understand, starting with the question of who you are, and why you are here, and how you broke through, and why you have come to challenge me.'

She spat that word at me, 'challenge', like I'd done something really terrible. 'No!' I actually gasped, horrified that she saw me as some kind of evil imposter, and scared of what she might do to me for being one. The way they were all so massively paranoid about outsiders 'breaking' in was seriously messed up. 'I haven't come to do anything. I don't *know* why I'm here.'

'Then tell me what you *do* know, girl.'

I told her everything I could remember, starting with the graveyard. She stopped me with another finger to my lips when I got to the part about the horses coming and me getting carried off by one of them and dumped where the girls found me.

'But I didn't send the horses.' She twitched her head so violently a coil of hair slipped free. 'And you say the black one came first, and then the white? That's the wrong order. It's always white first. Dawn, through day, to night. And I didn't bring the snow. First I shake out the snow, and then the horses come. I did neither. It wasn't time.'

I didn't know exactly what she meant by it, but her talking about *shaking* snow made me think of what Granny used to say about Lady Snowstorm shaking her skirts. I thought it was a character Granny had invented. Maybe it was from a story, but that still didn't explain why this old lady would 'shake' snow and then make horses come. With every passing minute, this place seemed even more bizarre.

'I have another question,' she said. 'A question relating to the theft.' She shuffled to the fireplace and rapped her nails on the steaming pot. 'Why did you steal the soup? How did you *know* about the soup?'

'I didn't steal it. One of the girls, Lola, brought it to Scarlet's last night. I was hungry, and I ate it, but I didn't steal it.'

'Scarlet knows about you? You were with her last night? What was she thinking? She should have brought you straight here. Has she lost her head from all that swinging around the wrong way up?'

I really didn't want to drop Scarlet in it, but what could I say? 'She was going to bring me to see you this morning. I went for a look around while I was waiting for her, and then your puppies . . .'

'Cubs,' she corrected. 'Wolf cubs.'

I couldn't believe it. *Wolves?* And they'd actually had their teeth in my dress. 'They're real wolves? Are they dangerous?'

'Yes, they are real wolves. But wait . . .' She crinkled her nose, which looked more like a beak than a nose. A sharp beak, covered in skin the texture of almonds. 'You said you were hungry. How could you be hungry?'

'The usual reason.' I shrugged. 'I needed food.'

'Tell me what happened. What was the cause? You haven't told me that.'

'Because I hadn't eaten for ages?' I hoped she didn't think I was being rude, but what else could I say?

'I mean, what is the cause of you being here? The death, child. The *death*.' Her chest rattled, and another coil of hair came loose. 'What was the cause of the death?'

'What? How do you know about Granny?'

'Granny? What granny? Was your grandmother with you when you came? Where is she now?'

I bit my lip, trying really hard not to get wound up by her speaking in riddles. It was maddening, like we were talking different languages. 'Nowhere. I mean, she's dead. She didn't come with me. It happened a few months ago. There was a fire.'

'Were you in this fire? Is that how you hurt your head? Is that what brought you here?'

'My head?' And then I wondered if the cut on my head *did* have something to do with me being here. I didn't know. Maybe I had an accident and couldn't remember exactly what had happened. Nothing made sense, and I started to shake and shake and it felt like the world was spinning out of control. Mother Matushka laid her hands on my shoulders. I winced, but she pressed harder and I could feel the warmth of her body and the smell of soil and salt coming from her, as if she was made from earth. I started to feel calmer and the shaking stopped. I let go of her, embarrassed that I'd been clinging onto her like she was someone I knew well enough to cling onto.

'What should I do?' I wiped my face. 'Can you help? Scarlet said you'd be able to help. It can't be far. My mum and dad will be out of their minds. How would you feel if your children didn't come home? Do you have children? Grandchildren?'

'I have many children. All creatures are my children, and you have broken into their home. You have disrupted our world.'

There it was again, them making it sound like I'd intruded on their secret cult. 'Where exactly am I?'

'Since you have already asked so many questions, and since there shall surely be many more, I very much need to drink some blue-rose brew. Fetch three heads for me. The most succulent you can find – if there *are* any succulent ones left.'

I suppose I could have just made a run for it right then, but I didn't. Something made me do as she asked, even though I couldn't see why me asking questions had anything to do with her needing to drink rose tea. Most of the blooms were withered, but I eventually found some healthier-looking buds.

'Rosie.' I felt a hand on my shoulder and jumped. My fingers slipped onto a thorn.

Scarlet pulled me round to face her. 'Why did you wander off like that? I was going to bring you. And what did Mother say? Does she know you stayed with me last night?'

I nodded, and felt my face reddening. I know I didn't really have anything to feel guilty about, but I didn't want to get her in any trouble.

'Sorry,' I said, but Scarlet wasn't listening to me. She was watching over my shoulder, eyes wide with fear.

'Oh Mother, I know I should've brought her straight to you when I saw her with Coco and Lola. I know, I know.'

Ignoring Scarlet, Mother Matushka took the roses from me and inspected them up close. 'Perfectly juicy and sweet,' she approved. 'I thought you'd destroyed them all.' Then she caught sight of my finger. 'Blood?' she spat, staring at it. '*Blood?*' She gave Scarlet a look.

'It's just from a thorn,' I said, but she ignored me too.

'And you didn't think this was important, Scarlet? Leave us. I shall see you later.'

She shut the door and nudged me inside, and I watched her pluck every petal from the three roses and put them in a mortar. Then she ground them into a bright blue paste and added some water, and I swear the veins on her arms and hands looked bluer once she'd drunk it down. I swear it looked as if the juice had run directly into her.

'That's better.' She smacked her lips. 'Questions age me, you see, but a drop of this puts me right. But things are not right, are they?' She made a high-pitched sucking sound, tongue against teeth. 'I *know* that your presence is disrupting the order, and what I do here is *keep* order. I perform a balancing act between life and death. I exist to help people pass through, and to uphold the boundaries between worlds.'

'What do you mean? Passing travellers? Scarlet said –'

'All that matters is what I say, child, not what Scarlet says,' she screeched. 'This is my world and you shouldn't be here.'

'I don't understand . . .'

'Do you understand *this*, child?' She was raging now, rearing back like a wild beast asserting power over its prey. As I jumped away from her, I swear I could see her bones through her skin and I swear that her hair was moving about her head and her teeth were clacking like they were made of metal. The overhead shelf started shaking and sent dozens of birds swooping down from the rafters. I ran to the door, but she got there first and went out with the birds swirling around her. She slammed it shut. I heard the iron lock snap down. I was locked in the cottage, like Gretel when the witch shut her up in the cage – only I didn't have Hansel, and there wasn't a cage, and this wasn't a story, and I didn't know what to do.

Chapter Twelve

I bashed and kicked against the door, yelling for Mother Matushka to let me out, screaming for Scarlet. My fists were sore and grazed and I felt like I was suffocating. I could hardly breathe. At first I thought it was due to all the bashing and panicking, but it wasn't just that. There was steam, or smoke, seeping through the spaces around the door. I screamed louder. Was she burning the cottage? Was she trying to *kill* me?

I frantically scanned the room for another way out. Maybe there was a back door I hadn't noticed, or a shuttered window – something, anything I might be able to escape through. But then, as I looked round the room, I saw that the smoke wasn't grey and there was no burning smell. It was white and vaporous, and the air was humid, not smoky. I laughed with relief. It was mist. It was like the mist that had closed in behind the sisters and me yesterday.

But that feeling of relief didn't last long. I wasn't going to die from smoke inhalation, but I was still trapped. Whenever I went near the door, more smothering vapours streamed in. If I retreated, the vapours thinned. So there *was* a cage, but made of mist, not bars, and I couldn't see a way out, and I didn't understand why I was being held prisoner by Mother Matushka.

That's what it was. I was her *prisoner*. And what was all that stuff about the sun and the animals? Why was she blaming me for whatever her problems were? The more I heard about this place, the more I thought it had to be some kind of secret sect, and that's why they called themselves 'the Unseen'. They wanted to keep themselves cut off from the outside world. I mean, what kind of circus was this? It didn't travel anywhere. There weren't any regular performances, and the only people who seemed to know about it were part of it.

There had to be another way out. There *had* to be. I explored every inch of the room. Mother Matushka didn't have many things, just the few pieces of furniture, the pot hanging over the fire and two buckets. One was filled with earth, the other with what looked like salt crystals. Then I found an ancient-looking instrument, a wing-shaped harp. I picked it up and it began to make a shimmery, chiming sound, like a creepy music box. I could see the strings moving as if someone was plucking them, but no one was. It stopped playing as soon as I put it down, like it could see me, or something. I know that sounds crazy, but it was like some strange magic was at work. Maybe their paranoia was rubbing off on me, but that's how it felt. I stepped away from it.

After feeling around all the walls a few times, and finding nothing, it struck me that there might be a way out through the roof. Maybe there was a gap around the spindle that poked through it. I looked up at the overhead shelf, thinking I could probably climb onto it. It wasn't very high. I was about to fetch a stool to try to pull myself up when I noticed that the shelf was connected to the spinning wheel by a chain. I pressed on the foot pedal and the chain unwound. As the shelf juddered down, something fell from it and landed at my feet. A Russian doll! I picked it up and stroked its shiny head. Another reminder of Granny. No, there were hundreds of reminders. The whole shelf was full of dolls, which made me smile. It was as if Granny had sent a whole army of little mother dolls to look after me – which I know sounds completely dumb, but it *was* uncanny to find them there.

I wound the shelf up a little and climbed onto it so I could get a look at the ceiling. The chain creaked and the platform wobbled, and I knocked more dolls to the floor. I gripped the chain to steady myself. I could almost touch the roof, but there was no gap around the spindle. I could feel my throat closing, like I was choking. There was no way out.

I don't know how much time had passed, but a while later the door was thrust open and Mother Matushka tumbled inside. I jumped to my feet. 'Can I go now? You really don't need to keep me here. I'm not here to do anything bad. Please.'

'Out of the way, girl!' she screeched. There was no oppressive mist, but she was engulfed in the same cluster of birds that had swept down from the roof. Their squawking was unbearably brutal, and the force from their flapping wings was so strong it felt like the cottage was revolving, with only the spoke of the spinning wheel pinning it down. She raised her arms and made a strange sign in the air with a finger. She did it again, and again. Frustrated, she cried out for the birds to come down and stop, but they didn't. It just got worse. They swarmed in and circled around me, transforming the cottage into a throbbing mass of feathers and beaks.

'Draw them down!' she screamed at me. 'Draw them down before they knock the shelf. Like this!' She made that sign with her finger again. It was a bit like a figure-of-eight loop. I didn't see how that would help, but she was screaming like our lives depended on it, so I did as she asked, as best as I could. It wasn't exactly easy to see anything through the chaos, and I had to keep covering my eyes to protect them, but I made that same loop with my finger, over and over again, and gradually the squawking and snapping faded to a gentle swishing. It became hypnotically regular, almost soothing, like lapping waves. I dared to raise my head. The birds were following the path of my finger, as if there was an invisible thread between us. I could feel it, too, like the thread really existed, like I was controlling a kite string, which in turn controlled hundreds of birds.

'Lead them out, steady and calm,' Mother Matushka instructed. 'Widen the loop to slow them down and send them away. I cannot keep them here in this state.'

She ushered me through the door and guided my arm to demonstrate what she meant, and together, somehow, we coaxed them to calmness and, through drawing an increasingly larger loop with our united arm, we made them vanish beyond the horizon.

'What children would turn on their mother?' she murmured, and I actually felt sorry for her. It was like she really believed they'd betrayed her. 'May you return to me as you were,' she called after them.

After that, neither of us spoke for some time. We both caught our breath, and I don't know about Mother Matushka, but I was also drinking in the silence. It was like the beautiful coolness that comes after a summer thunderstorm, and I felt really alive, all clean and refreshed.

'What *was* that?' I whispered. 'Is that normal? I never knew I could do anything like that. I mean, I didn't know it was possible to control things like that. It was incredible. How does it work?'

Mother Matushka didn't reply. She looked drained, and that fiery, gold glint in her eyes had faded a little. She set about making herself more blue rose tea.

'I'll do that,' I offered.

Mother Matushka looked at me through narrowed eyes, all wary and distrustful, but she took the cup from me and raised it to her lips. As I watched her gulp it down so greedily, my stomach made a massive growling noise.

'You are hungry? I thought you already ate my soup.'

'I did, but that was a while ago, wasn't it?'

'One serving should be enough, girl. It usually is.' She went to the pot and served me a bowl. I hadn't thought about food until now, but I slurped it down like I hadn't eaten for a week. Maybe the tea had invigorated her, or maybe the frailty she'd shown was a just a tiny, temporary moment of weakness, but as I finished the last drop, Mother Matushka pounced across the room.

'What have you done?' she screeched, gathering the dolls from the floor. 'Is that why you're here? You have come to tamper with the Soul Mothers? Did you open them? Tell me the truth, girl. The truth!'

I shrank back, shaking my head. This was crazier than ever. I mean, I could understand someone being annoyed about their stuff being messed around with, but her reaction was way beyond annoyed.

'Sorry. They fell off the shelf. They're not broken. I'm sure they're not.' But she clearly didn't believe me. She checked each one in turn, from the base to the head, taking extra care over examining the split around their bellies.

'What else have you meddled with, girl?' She got down on her knees in front of the fire and pulled on a ring that was fixed to one of the floorboards. A panel of wood opened. She let it slam down flat and I could have kicked myself for not thinking of checking the floor as well as the ceiling. A wall of icy air blasted from the pit she'd exposed and I could see it was full of more dolls, hundreds of them.

'Did you open the hatch, girl? Did you take any from here?'

'I didn't even know this opened. I knocked them off the shelf. I'm sorry, I didn't mean . . .'

'It must be sealed. Everything must be sealed.' Mother Matushka shut the trapdoor and scattered a handful of salt and earth around its edge. 'Quickly, child. Do as I'm doing.'

While I followed her lead, pressing salt and earth into the crack around the hatch and the hearth, wondering why the hell we were doing it, I thought of what Mum had said about the devil and bad luck. Maybe she should have thrown the whole cellar over her shoulder.

And then something shot into my head and I had to sit down.

Seeing Mother Matushka there in the hearth made me think about Granny, and the tin I'd found in *her* hearth. I must have blanked it out, I don't know, but until now, until seeing Mother Matushka like this, I'd forgotten about that heart-stabbing letter that said Granny had *meant* to die. And then my mind started racing. I wondered if Mum had found it, and I hated to think what that was doing to her on top of me being gone. Maybe Mum thought that's *why* I was gone. *Jesus.* I swallowed hard. What if that did have something to do with it? What if that *was* the reason? That was the last thing I remembered before being here. Maybe I totally lost it and ran off and somehow ended up stumbling into this place. I don't know. My vision blurred and I was filled by a terrible, gut-wrenching longing to be back with Mum, arguing about the necklace and finding out about Granny's secret life.

'I think I know what happened,' I blurted.

'What is it, girl?' asked Mother Matushka. 'What do you know?'

I spilled it all out. I told her exactly what happened with Granny and the fire, and then finding her letter.

'I need to go home to Mum and Dad. Why can't I just

go? Why has this happened to *me*? Why are you keeping me locked up here?'

Mother Matushka inhaled deeply, like she was sucking all the air from the room. 'I must go to the Big Top. I must find the answers.'

She left me alone again, and I heard the door lock, again, but this time Mother Matushka hadn't turned into an ogress, all sharp teeth and fiery eyes and bones about to break through her skin. This time I felt a pang of hope. She said she would find the answers. That had to offer *some* hope, didn't it?

As she walked, Mother Matushka went over what she knew. The girl had come through the seal from the outside, which explained the unsettled animals and the struggle with the sun. But the birds had gone to the girl, not to *her*. It was the girl who'd controlled them and drawn them down. So she had restored order, as well as disrupted it. *And would someone seeking to disrupt my world make tea to restore me?* she thought. *And would they express such a strong desire to go home?*

Of course, Matushka had seen many newcomers struggle to accept what had happened to them. She had seen scores attempt to leave, either hungry to return to wherever they'd come from, or even desperate to go through, hoping to end what they thought they couldn't bear. But, in time, everyone found their place here. They came to accept their condition, and they found things to enjoy, and things they were good at, and the desire to leave slipped away, like a serpent through wet hands, and the Circus became more than something to bear. It became a place in which they could do things they'd never dared do, a place in which they could become whatever they wanted to be.

Matushka could see this girl wasn't like the others, but she was here, and now, to her relief, she had some inkling as to why she'd come. The hearth she'd mentioned was clearly the reason for her arrival, and Mother knew she would uncover the details in time. That was often the case. Newcomers took time to voice what had happened to them. They couldn't say the words, because saying the words made it true. But for now, the girl being here was a fact, and that had to be accepted. *Shouldn't this girl be given the same chance as the others?* she wondered. *Shouldn't she also be sent to the Big Top to find her way?*

Mother Matushka's performers parted a way for her as she passed through them. None dared ask about the unexpected arrival, none voiced their fear, but she sensed it. It was there in the playing of her musicians. It was there in the twirls of her dancers, the somersaults of the tumblers and, strongest of all, it was there in Lola's refusal to meet her eye. She beckoned her over.

'It wasn't my fault,' said Lola. 'We didn't go too far, we really didn't, and I wanted to bring her straight to you, but Scarlet . . .'

'Just tell me what you know, child. Tell me all that you saw, and all that you know.'

Mother Matushka listened calmly until Lola mentioned the marsh. Hearing how it had retreated around the girl, and how the waters had run clear, sent shockwaves through her. The marsh had been here as long as her. In the beginning, before any people passed through, there was Mother Matushka, and there was the mist and there was the marsh. That's how it was, that's how it had always been. And the girl had *changed* it, and when things change, they can never go back as they were.

'She said she didn't do anything, but I saw it happen. We both did. You can ask Coco if you don't believe me. Who is she, Mother? It's her fault everything has gone funny, isn't it? Has she upset you?'

Mother Matushka placed a hand on Lola's shoulder to calm her. The girl was shaking. She couldn't let this fear spread among her children. They needed to feel safe. Some order had to be maintained. 'What about the mist, my child? Was that as it should be?'

Lola nodded. 'It was just the marsh she made change. She stepped into it and started to drown, but then it just shrank away from her. Why has the sun been funny, Mother? Was that the girl's fault too?'

'I shall see, child. I shall see who she is, and what she can do, like the rest of you.'

Chapter Thirteen

The door opened. I sat up, still half in my dream. In it, I'd been back at home, in my room in the cellar – only Scarlet and Fabian had been there too, and we'd found another envelope of Granny's things, more pieces to her puzzle.

'Stir yourself, girl. You're leaving.'

'What?'

Mother Matushka's words catapulted me awake. I didn't know what to do with myself. I wanted to laugh and cry and dance and even hug her. 'I'd like to say goodbye to Scarlet first.'

'No need for goodbyes. You'll see her soon enough. Her and all the others. Accordienka, we're ready,' she called. 'She will take you to the Big Top. Her father will be your guide there. I shall find you later.'

I felt totally flattened. I shouldn't have let myself get carried away like that. 'Why do I have to go there?'

'I know how the marsh shrank back for you, and I saw for myself how the birds came to you, so let us see how you fare in the Circus of the Unseen.'

'What do you mean?' I asked. The thought of being forced

to do some kind of circus act as a test turned my stomach.

'Let us see what you can do,' she said. 'Let us see what you learn,' she went on, which didn't help me at all. She blew onto one of the skull-capped fence-posts and a flame ignited. She uprooted the whole post and handed it to me. 'In case you need to light your way; in case the sun fails. But do not stray from any path,' she warned, as if she knew what I was thinking. 'All paths return to me.'

Accordienka took my hand, like I was the little sister she'd been told to take care of, and the wind whipped up and jostled us away. I just kept telling myself, over and over, to stay calm and sharp and not fall to pieces. What else could I do? At least I wasn't locked up. I glanced back at the cottage, with its stilts and skulls and the blast of blue roses round the door, and I saw Mother Matushka flapping her arms at the sky, and I swear it looked like she was making the wind herself. As Accordienka led me to the crossroads, that familiar mist closed in around us.

'Is the weather always so strange here?' I asked. 'It's like you have your own climate.'

She didn't reply to that, or to any of my questions, like why I had to go to the Big Top, and what I was supposed to do there, and if she'd always lived here. She just looked at me with her big, dark eyes, as if she was speaking, but no words came. I don't know if Mother Matushka had told her to keep quiet, or if she was shy, or maybe she just didn't like me because I'd gone to pick up her doll, but she didn't say a single word. I almost jumped out of my skin when someone else did.

'Pleased to meet you, missy. Welcome to my water wagon.'

I'd been babbling on so much, hoping Accordienka would respond to *something*, that I hadn't noticed him, or where we were. The person was an old boatman who looked as beaten up by the elements as his canoe. We'd come to a lake that was so clear and calm, it looked like a perfect disc of polished glass. He tipped his hat at us.

'Is this what we're supposed to be doing?' I asked Accordienka. 'Mother Matushka said I had to go to the Big Top.'

The boatman released a rough, crackly laugh. 'Ain't nobody told you, missy? She ain't said a word since the day she and her daddy came to be here. But you speak through your music, don't you, girl? You speak through your bellows rather than your mouth.'

So that explained why she hadn't answered me. She *couldn't* speak. Before I could ask why, Accordienka climbed aboard. The boatman must have sensed my fear, because he took the skull from me and lifted me on. Then he paddled away, singing out in a graveyard-gravelly voice that came deep from his belly.

The river don't stop, and the river don't rest.
The river keeps a-flowing when there's no flesh left.
The earth don't rot and the earth don't rust.
The earth keeps a-swelling when your bones are dust.
Got to flow with the river, got to keep flowing higher.
Got to ride that river right back to the mire.

His haunting, hypnotic song mixed with the rhythm of the oars sloshing into the water and the ripples lapping against the boat, and I felt adrift from everything – until the lapping and chanting stopped. We'd come to land.

After helping me out, the boatman handed me the skull-post, wished me well and rowed off. I followed Accordienka up over the rocky bank beyond the shoreline. It was packed with hundreds of fossilised shells, like the ghost town of a reef. At the highest point, I could see the Big Top's candy-striped canopy jutting out of the valley. Accordienka waved at her father and Scarlet, and I raced after her down the bank towards them.

'I hope I didn't get you in any trouble with Mother Matushka,' I said to Scarlet.

'Don't worry about that. It could have been worse. She has other things on her mind.'

I guessed the 'other things' were me. I wanted to ask them why I'd been locked up, and about Mother's crazy reaction to the dolls, and what had happened with the birds, but the noise coming from inside the tent was too loud to start up a big conversation.

'So this is the Place of the Players,' Fabian called, lifting Accordienka onto his shoulders like she weighed no more than a feather. 'Mother asked that I introduce you to what we do here.'

Scarlet took the skull-post from me and jabbed it into the ground. 'Welcome to the World, honey!' She flipped back the curtain, put an arm round me and shepherded me inside. It *was* like being in a different world. It looked even bigger from the inside. The canopy glowed silver, like it was flooded with moonlight.

'Where shall we start?' said Fabian. 'See there?' He gestured upwards. 'That's Henri, and the smaller one is Jacques. They're brothers – the Tremendous Tightrope Walkers of Toulouse. They are called that because they can walk the branches of the highest trees, and because –'

'They're from Toulouse?'

'You might think so.' He winked. 'But not exactly. Sometimes they are from Toulouse. Other times they are from Tonga, or some other place. It depends on their mood. They are whoever, or whatever, they want to be.' Then, gently, Fabian lifted Accordienka from his shoulders to the ground. She hurried away and came back soon with her accordion. Sitting down, she began to play.

The two boys in matching sailors' outfits and wolf masks were balanced at either end of a tightrope. They bowed to each other before taking tiny, exact steps across the wire towards the centre until the tips of their noses touched. Then, while one of them stayed completely still, the other rotated his arms forward and somersaulted over his brother's head. He hovered several metres above him for what felt like an age. I could hardly bear to watch. There was no net beneath them and what he was doing seemed impossible. I mean, how was he holding himself in that position for so long? It was crazy. But then things became even crazier. They began to howl like they actually were wolves, and I saw them sprout tails and bristles that burst through their clothes.

'Is this really happening?' I breathed. 'Can you see it too?'

'Quick, don't miss Dolly Dimple.' Scarlet nudged me. 'She's our Mistress of the Midair Marvel!' She pointed across the ring at a plump lady dressed in a snakeskin-print leotard and bathing cap. The lady smeared grease over the bare bits of her body, climbed a set of steps up to a cannon and somehow managed to squeeze herself into it. Just thinking about how she could breathe in such a tiny space made my chest tight. A small boy wearing a harlequin suit tumbled over to the cannon and wound a handle at one end. A click-clack-clicking sound started up, and then came a big bang and a cloud of smoke and Dolly Dimple shot out of the other end towards a water-filled glass tank. She vanished on contact with the water, but the tank now contained a poisonous-looking snake-like creature. I knew it was behind glass, but just seeing its yellow-green slithers sent shivers through me, and I *swear* it hadn't been there before. I swear the tank had been empty before the woman plunged into it.

There were things like this going on across the entire ring. I watched a group of female fire-eaters slip flaming torches down their throats and engulf themselves in flames. They flapped and beat their arms a few times and a flock of orange birds emerged from the blaze. I saw a woman walk right through a mirror and come out the other side as a man, but the most bizarre – and disturbing – thing of all was watching a boy being gagged and nailed into a coffin. A few seconds later, the coffin burst open and a cluster of spiders, each as big as a dinner plate, scurried from it, and there was no boy.

All this was more incredible than anything I'd seen in any

other circus, or on any illusion show. It was more incredible than anything I'd imagined possible. But, actually, what made their acts even *more* spectacular was the way they performed them. Despite all the chaotic movements and the colour and noise, there was a grace to everything the performers did – all their moves were considered, and executed with dignity. The atmosphere was solemn, and underpinned by Accordienka's drone.

'Are you *her*?' It was one of the wolf brothers. I hadn't seen them change back, but they both looked like normal boys again. '*Are* you her?' he shouted again, and right in my face this time, so close I could feel his cold breath on my cheeks. 'Are you the one Lola found?'

At those words, everyone around us stopped what they were doing. They stopped and they stared and they gathered around me. The red-and-white harlequin tumblers, the women in cheetah-print bodysuits, the boys dressed as foxes. I couldn't speak, and it felt like a thousand eyes were staring at me. Accordienka ran to her dad and clung onto his legs. I moved closer to him too.

'Please, step away,' Fabian called at the crowd, but they babbled over him.

'Who is she? Where did she come from? What is she doing here? What is she *for*?' Then they turned their questions onto me. 'What happened to you?' Another voice: 'Are you still hungry? Do you really bleed?' Another: 'Can you feel this?' A woman dressed as a pink flamingo leaned in and went to pinch me, like I was an exhibit in a freak show.

I went to say something, but Fabian nudged her away

and touched my arm to keep me quiet. 'That is enough,' he shouted. 'Enough!'

'It is her. I found her.' It was Lola. 'And she does bleed. I saw it.'

'Stop tormenting her, Lola. She is but a child.'

'So am I,' said Lola. 'So are lots of us. It's all her fault. The sun, the marsh. She's made everything messy. I know because Mother spoke to me about her.'

'Get back to your work! All of you. I, also, have spoken to Mother Matushka and she said that this girl is to come here and learn with us. This is not for you to meddle in, Lola, or any of you.'

Their protests faded to murmurs and everyone went back to what they'd been doing, and I could breathe again.

'Let's find some quiet,' said Fabian, leading me outside, and we went away from the Big Top to where he and Accordienka lived. It wasn't far, but their shady clearing near the lake couldn't have felt more different. The peace and the way the light fell on the lake was one of the most beautiful things I'd ever seen. We sat on a bench outside their hut while Accordienka played near the shore.

'Thank you,' I said. 'If you hadn't stopped them, I don't know what they'd have done.'

'It won't happen again, I'll make sure of it,' he replied. 'And I wanted to say that I didn't mean you are a child. You are a young woman. I meant you are a child in this place and they should not have treated you like that. I am sorry.'

I could feel myself blushing, but he didn't seem to notice.

'Their reaction was because they do not know you,' he went

on, 'because you are from the outside. Of course, new people come here, but we always know when. It is never like this. Usually new arrivals who stay are welcomed with a show.'

'Can everyone here do illusions like that?' I asked. 'I mean, turn themselves into animals, and escape from coffins. How did they do it?'

'That's what they have learned to do here. Everyone finds their own special abilities.'

'What do you do?' I asked. 'What's your act?'

'Sometimes I am the Fabulous Fabianski, and other times I am Fabian of the Forest. When I am either, I do things with my hands. I move things and I catch things and I make things, like this house of ours, Scarlet's wagon, Wheels of Death, dolls. Anything we need. Accordienka!' he called to his daughter. 'Why don't you play something for our guest?'

'I'd love that,' I said. She was such a sweet little thing. It was amazing she was strong enough to hold the instrument, let alone play it so brilliantly. She settled on a stone near the lake's edge and closed her eyes. The sounds she made were so achingly beautiful I actually started crying. It felt like her music was literally moving through me, swelling my heart. She must have noticed, because she put down the accordion and ran up to me. She wiped away my tears, and gently pulled my lips into a smile.

'Mama!' she said, pointing right into my face.

'*Darling?*' Fabian cried. 'You spoke! Did you really speak?'

'Mama!' she said again, then raced inside the hut and returned waggling her doll, saying something in a language I couldn't understand.

Fabian lifted her up. He was sparkling more than the sun on the lake. He pulled her close, with tears running down his cheeks. 'This is the first time she has spoken since we came here.'

'What did she say?'

'She said that I made the doll, and her mama painted it. She also said you look like her mother. Perhaps it's your eyes.' He glanced at me, then pulled Accordienka close. 'I never thought I'd hear her voice again. Thank you, Rosie. Somehow, you have given my daughter her voice back.'

I didn't know about that, but I did want to know how a person could just lose their voice. I mean, I thought you were born mute and that was that. I didn't think voices could just go.

'What made her stop speaking?'

'It was the shock of being without her mother and twin. Sorry . . .' He broke off, choked up. 'I cannot . . . Even after all these years I can find it difficult to speak about what happened. But still, we are together here, and you, Accordienka, have found your voice!' He hugged her tight. 'Let's go back. I want everyone to know; I want everyone to hear her.'

He turned to go, but I couldn't bring myself to follow. I really didn't want to leave. I felt safe here with him, away from the others.

'Don't be frightened.' He linked arms with me. 'Don't let their fear upset you. Scarlet and I will look out for you. You can't hide away here forever.'

Fabian's words made me think of what Granny had said

about not letting fear stop me from doing things, so I went with them, but with a new, unfamiliar twist in my heart. Fabian's words about his wife and other daughter had really affected me. I'd seen something new here. I'd seen that these people, or Fabian at least, cared about the lives they'd lived and people they'd loved *before* they came to the circus. I mean, he knew what it was to miss people, and he knew of a world outside, which gave me some hope that he'd understand why I had to go home.

Chapter Fourteen

When we returned to the Big Top and Fabian told them their news, everyone flocked around Accordienka. I was so happy for her, of course I was, but honestly, I think I was even happier I wasn't the centre of attention. They were only interested in hearing Accordienka for themselves. I slipped into a seat at the side of the ring, feeling massively relieved that no one seemed to have noticed me at all, until Coco called out to me, and I felt all eyes on me again.

'You must be magic, Rose Girl! Did you make her speak?'

'*Did* you?' demanded Lola.

Everyone's stare moved from me to the highest point of the Top. Lola and Coco were up there in a birdcage, hanging upside down by their spindly legs, like feathery bats. Coco slipped off the bar and leapt out. My stomach jumped into my mouth as I rushed to where she might land. There was nothing beneath her, nothing to catch her, nothing to soften her fall. But then something crazy happened. After plummeting a few metres, she spread her arms wide and floated the rest of the way down. The sleeves of her feathered dress seemed to work as wings. She landed with a giggle right next to me. Her little face was almost as wrinkled as Mother Matushka's, but her eyes were bright. She plucked a feather from her dress and offered it to me.

'This is for you, Rose Girl,' she said. 'A magic feather.'

She might have been one of the youngest people I'd seen here, but she was the least afraid of me, the least hostile, and her being so kind made a big, dry lump rise to my throat. I tried to push back the crying, but I couldn't.

'Don't cry. I didn't mean to make you cry. I'm your friend. Are you my friend?' She crinkled her nose, and I thought she was about to cry too.

'Course I'm your friend,' I replied.

The next thing I knew, I was surrounded by people again, all reaching out to touch me, and this time I didn't have Fabian to protect me. I couldn't even see him. Lola appeared at the front of the crowd. 'Did you make her speak?' she demanded again.

'I don't think so. I don't see how I could have. She did it herself. I just happened to be there, like everything else. I didn't mean to do anything with the marsh either, I didn't mean to do anything.'

'But why are you here? Why did you come?'

'And what can you do?' asked the smaller of the wolf boys. 'What's so special about you?'

'What do you mean? I'm not special.'

'Jacques means that everyone here can do something,' his brother explained.

'Me and Lolly make music,' said Coco, and to prove it she sang out in an incredible voice that sounded like hundreds of different birds, all singing at once in their own distinct way.

'Let's see if you can balance,' said Henri. 'Mother said you're supposed to learn with us, so let's see if you can do that.'

He positioned two barrels a few metres apart and laid a plank between them. Then he leapt onto the plank and turned a few somersaults. 'The trick to good balance is to fix your eyes on an invisible point directly in front of you. Keep your chin level, and keep your back straight, like this,' he demonstrated. 'It helps if you imagine the whole world is at your feet. Take hold of me.'

I went to take his hand, but faltered. They must have all seen how nervous I was. I mean, I hated heights, and just the thought of performing in front of all these people was making me dizzy.

'Give it a go, girl. Don't be scared.' Hearing Scarlet's voice gave me a little confidence. I mean, I felt I could trust her to make sure they didn't do anything bad to me, and the plank *was* just a metre or so off the ground, and even a person who hated heights shouldn't be scared of that. I reached for Henri's hand and stepped up.

'That's it, honey. Walk the wire, don't look down!' Scarlet called.

Slowly, I drew up my other leg and felt a wave of relief. My knees were trembling like mad, but I was actually standing on the plank! I knew it was nothing to write home about, but I was up there. Feeling a bit more assured, and encouraged by Scarlet's squeals, I took a few shaky steps forward. But then, as I smiled at her, internally congratulating myself on the dubious accomplishment of wobbling along a plank, I slipped and fell into one of the barrels, only to find it was full of murky water. I spluttered to the surface with hair plastered all over my face and my dress stuck to my skin.

'Hopeless,' laughed Jacques. 'You're far too wobbly. And weak.'

'Don't listen to him.' It was Fabian. He came to my rescue by lifting me from the barrel. 'You have showed great strength, Rosie. You have shown spirit.'

I pulled back my hair and plumped out my wet dress, desperately hoping it hadn't turned see-through. But the funny thing was, even though I felt like a complete clown, and even though this had been worse than all the disastrous audition scenarios I'd imagined that had crippled me since that time I'd frozen on stage – things like freezing again, tripping up, going on stage with my skirt tucked into my knickers, or naked – I felt pretty amazing that I'd given this a go. Yes, I'd cocked up, but I had nothing else to lose now, and I actually felt excited. Granny was right about trying being better than doing nothing.

'So what *can* she do?' Lola looked to Fabian for an answer.

'I suppose she can do many things, and I suppose she shall learn to do many things, if she stays with us, for isn't that what happens? Isn't that what happened to you? You were not always the famous high-flying singers, Miss Lola Lemona and Coco Coo. You were not always able to become two little songbirds, and I was not always able to do what I do.'

His words got me even more wound up about learning to do something 'special', as that wolf boy had put it. I wasn't deluded enough to think I'd suddenly transform into the greatest tightrope walker the world had ever seen, but there had to be something I could make my 'thing'.

'What about you?' I asked Fabian. 'Show me your act.'

'Very well,' he replied, rubbing his hands together. When he opened them, there was a little ball of fire throbbing in his palms. He threw it into the air and it split into more balls. He caught each one as it cascaded down and juggled with them. 'Ludo!' he called. 'Let us perform the biting of the bullets!'

The harlequin boy who'd lit Dolly Dimple's cannon ran over to a trunk and returned with a gun. 'Let us play!' he cried with a bow, then he raised his arms and pointed the gun at Fabian. I clenched my fists tight. The blast of the first bullet made me jump. Then another came, and another. It happened so fast, but I felt like I was seeing it in slow motion – Fabian catching a whole spray of bullets between his teeth, all the while keeping the flaming balls in the air. He had a smile on his face the whole time too, like this was nothing, like he hadn't even needed to concentrate.

'That's incredible,' I gasped. 'I mean, *really* incredible.'

'That's nothing,' said Jacques. 'You should see him become the Beast Who Walks Like a Man. Show her the bear, Fabian.'

My heart flipped. 'You can turn into a bear?' I asked. 'Like the boys become wolves?' But, actually, the thing that shocked me even more than the thought of Fabian turning into a bear was how Jacques had described it. *The Beast Who Walks Like a Man* – that's what Granny had called the story about Mashenka and the bear and the basket of pies. I'd never seen it in any books. I'd only ever heard her mention it.

'Now is not the time for transformations, Jacques. Now is the time to prepare for the sun setting and resting. You will stay here tonight, Rosie, with the others. Coco, will you show Rosie where to go?'

'Can't I stay with you?' I asked, disappointed I couldn't go with him and Accordienka to their peaceful hut near the lake. 'Or Scarlet? What if they turn on me again?'

'This is Mother's wish,' he said.

'And nearly all of us sleep around the Big Top,' said Coco. '*I* do.'

'Outside?' I asked.

She nodded. 'Don't be scared. You can lie near me.' She slipped her hand into mine and we filed from the Top. I felt like Fabian had deserted me, but I had to snap out of feeling sorry for myself. I had to keep my guard up. In all the excitement of being in the Big Top, I'd almost forgotten what I was supposed to be doing. I had to stay focused on finding a way to leave. We settled down outside with the others.

'How long have you been in the circus?' I asked. 'Are your mum and dad here?'

'Oh, no,' she said. 'They're probably still on the island, or maybe they went back to London. We left them ages ago. That's why we're here. We left and we drowned and then we woke up in the circus.'

I couldn't hide my shock. In that single sentence she'd said

126

far too much for my brain to process. 'You *drowned*? And you woke up here? I don't understand, Coco. How did that happen?' And my mind was also racing at her mention of London. She knew London! Maybe I wasn't that far from the world I knew.

'How did we drown? Me and Lolly took a boat out to sea and it capsized and we went under the water, that's how, silly. Lolly says we should never have gone to live on the island, but Daddy said we had to because we had no money, and people used to call us names.' She wrinkled her nose. 'Do you think we look like monsters? That's what they used to call us, because we look like this, because we look old. But we can't help it. We got old really quickly, when we were babies, and none of the doctors knew what to do with us. But we didn't have enough money to pay for them anyway. That's why Daddy took us to the island.'

It hurt to hear how they'd been treated for the way they looked, and then an awful thought flashed into my head. Maybe that's why they were here, in the circus. I didn't think that kind of thing still happened.

'Well, I think you're lovely.' And I meant it, but I also felt a twinge of guilt about the look of horror I'd had on my face when I'd first seen her and Lola. I hoped they hadn't noticed. 'Have you seen your mum and dad since you came here? Have they visited you? Is the island far from here, or London?'

'We can't see them, silly. And the island is *miles* away.'

Coco told me it had taken them months to sail across the sea to their new home in the Caribbean, where their parents worked in the household of the island's governor. It sounded pretty incredible – they'd lived in the grounds of his fancy house, surrounded by lush flowers and exotic birds and butterflies – but I was wondering where this was leading. I mean, how had they ended up in the Circus of the Unseen, so far from their mum and dad?

'Mr Governor didn't mind us looking old and wrinkly,' Coco went on. 'He said it was because we were special, but when he was bitten by a snake in his own garden and died from the poison, Mrs Governor said it was our fault. She called us "ungodly creatures" and said we'd put a curse on their house. Then she threw us out and we had nowhere to live and Daddy couldn't get a new job because she'd made everyone believe we were bad. But then Lolly had an idea. She said if we left Mummy and Daddy, they'd be all right because everyone blamed us, not them. So that's why she rowed us out to sea, to find our own island to live on, but the waves were really big and strong and the boat tipped up and we drowned.'

I didn't know what to think. I felt so angry that someone – was it Mother Matushka? Lola? – must have fed her this crazy story as the truth. 'Are you sure, Coco? How did you get here?'

'Because we died between the sea and the sky, and between the water and the earth, silly. Mother Matushka said that's what makes us special, and that's why we woke up here. I was sad at first, but it's better than just being dead, isn't it? We didn't do flying before we came here, so being here might even be better than being alive.'

'Oh, Coco.' I stroked her hair. She really was breaking my heart. I wondered if their parents had died and she was confused, or had been told the wrong thing. 'That's a funny thing to say. I think you might be mixed up.'

She cocked her head at me. 'You've only just arrived here, haven't you? Me and Lolly have been here for about one hundred years.' She looked at me with her piercing blue eyes. 'You still want to go home, don't you? I wanted to at first, but now I like it here. I still love Mummy and Daddy though, and just because we're not with them doesn't mean we don't love them. But I think you should stop wanting to go home. If you keep wanting to go home, and if you try to leave, you'll only end up like Freddie. Don't do that, Rose Girl. I wouldn't want that to happen to you.'

I'd heard that name before. Scarlet had mentioned him when I first arrived. 'What happened to Freddie?'

She leaned in close to me. 'If I tell you, it has to be our secret. Do you promise to keep the secret?'

'I promise.'

'He's a naughty boy who kept trying to escape, so Mother locked him in a cave over that way.' She pointed. 'It's near the waterfall behind the Big Top.' She covered my mouth with a cold hand. 'Shh, Rose Girl! You mustn't tell anyone I told you, especially not Mother Matushka and *especially* not Lola.'

Just then, all the flames on the skull-posts around the Big Top died. All of them, I noticed, except for the one closest to the opening of the tent, the one I'd carried here. That one still flickered and, in its glow, I watched the performers lie down. 'What's happening now? Is this where we're supposed to sleep?'

'We don't exactly sleep,' said Coco. 'We lie down and rest until Mother comes again to do the light. We don't need to sleep, but she says we need to have a night and a day. She's going to make the night now, look.'

Mother Matushka was standing in front of the entrance to the Big Top. She looked more ancient than ever, like one of those bodies preserved in a bog. Her skin was shiny, leathery meat, shrouded in fur. She stretched out her arms and performed the same ritual I'd seen outside the cottage, only this time, after grasping the invisible wheel, she turned it anti-clockwise. The sun moved quickly at first, but she faltered, and it seemed to get stuck just over the Big Top, like it was burning into the canopy.

I still couldn't believe this was real. How could it be? The trappings of an illusion *had* to be somewhere. I watched Mother Matushka straining, putting the full force of her body into turning the wheel, and then, with one last almighty effort, the sun jerked down and a thin blade of moon emerged over the edge of the rocky verge that lay beyond the trees that ringed the Big Top. Then she picked up a pail and went into those trees, scattering something as she went.

I turned on my side to face Coco. She was lying down flat, completely still, completely silent, but with her eyes wide open. All the others I could see looked the same, like they were in a trance, somewhere between sleep and wakefulness. There were no breathing sounds, no sleep snuffles or snores, and in the moonlight their skin looked like stone. I couldn't sleep here. It was like lying with the dead. And I had this horrible creeping feeling that this circus wasn't actually part of the world I knew. No, it was more than creeping. The sense that there was too much madness going on here for it to be a weird secret sect was starting to *flood* through me.

And as well as the freakiness of Mother Matushka appearing to make night and day, and Coco talking about dying, and the weird horses and birds and ghostly instruments that played themselves, there were also the connections with Granny, like the dolls, and that wolf boy mentioning *The Beast Who Walked Like a Man*. I couldn't just lie here doing nothing. If that boy, Freddie, had tried to leave, maybe he knew something. I had to find him, and I couldn't wait.

Chapter Fifteen

I waved my hand in front of Coco's face, to be certain she couldn't see. The last thing I needed was anyone trying to stop me, or worse. I did the same to the person lying the other side of me, the flamingo girl who'd tried to pinch me. Neither of them showed any response, so I took the lit skull-post and left.

Even with the torch, I couldn't see further than a few metres ahead, but the darkness made my hearing hypersensitive. I could hear the tiniest movements in the bushes and grass – scratches, shuffles, whirrs and crunches – and I tried not to imagine what creatures might be making them.

I pressed on in the direction Coco had pointed to, feeling increasingly stupid about this whole 'plan'. Her gesture had been pretty vague and even if I found this Freddie boy, what good would it do? And, in all likelihood, he was probably as real as Coco's story about what had happened to her and Lola. I kind of believed parts of it, like them being bullied – but everything else? Maybe there was some truth in it, but I didn't think I'd heard the *whole* truth.

The flame flickered in the wind, so I cupped my free hand

around it and turned onto a more protected-looking route, through more tightly clustered trees, to keep it alight. It wasn't long before I found myself close to the rocky bank Accordienka and I had climbed down to get into the circus area. I noticed an opening in the rocks, and my heart leapt. Maybe this was the cave Coco meant. If that existed, maybe the boy did too. The opening was nothing more than a narrow split, just wide enough for me to slip through. The air inside made my chest tighten. It was stiflingly humid, like when you step off the plane after landing in a hot country or visit a tropical greenhouse in a nature park, and I was standing on soft, red clay, with wet stonework either side of me and overhead. The narrow entryway had opened out into a huge cave. A gust of wind whipped through the opening, and my flame went out. I froze in the pitch-blackness, listening to the drip-drip-drip of water and feeling the occasional splat smack me on my bare shoulders. As I crept forward, a rush of water joined the drips and their echoes. The waterfall had to be through here. 'Hello!' I called. 'Freddie?' As I crept on, slow and cautious, the noise became violently loud. Even if the boy *was* here, he probably couldn't hear me. I went deeper into the cave, feeling my way along the wet walls to the source of the noise. Cold water sprayed my face and the sound was now deafening. I had reached the deepest part of the cave. I'd walked the whole way through, and found no one. Coco must have got it wrong, or maybe Freddie was in a different cave. Maybe there were others along the bank.

Just as I was about to turn back, I noticed spots of light

catching on the cascading water, occasionally sparkling like little crystals. And, through the gaps in its flow, I could see that the cave continued beyond the waterfall. I *hadn't* yet reached the deepest point. 'One, two, three,' I counted and ran through the stream. It thrashed down hard on my head and back. The air this side of the water was cold, and the ground and walls were crumbly and left salty traces on my wet body. As I wiped it from my arms and legs, the saltiness turned to misty vapours that rose and swirled above me. I stared up at them, mesmerised, but lost my balance and slipped against something. There was a smashing sound. I cried out as a spike of glass pierced the palm of my right hand, and one, two, three, four, five lights flashed on right in front of me. And then I saw the boy.

Only it wasn't a boy. It was a dusty statue of a boy's head inside a broken glass case. The head looked like it had been burned and frozen, like someone preserved at Pompeii. As I touched it, its eyes flashed open and its mouth released a gasp of air. I screamed and jumped back.

'You took your time,' said the head.

Keeping my distance, I tiptoed around it. The glass case was sitting on top of a large wooden box. It was like one of those creepy fortune-tellers' cabinets you find at the seaside – stick in a coin for it to spit out a cryptic one-liner about your future – except this was even creepier. This was a talking, dead-looking child's head, with no slots, and no wires.

'Cat got your tongue?' it asked. 'I *said*, you took your time. Did Mother Matushka send you? Are you going to unfreeze the rest of me? Been here long enough, haven't I? Must've been punished enough by now. Come clean, girl, she sent you, didn't she?'

'She didn't send me,' I replied, almost laughing at myself. Was I actually having a conversation with a mechanical head?

'Thinking about it, I might just believe you. Mother wouldn't have sent someone else to do her work. Likes to keep things in her control, doesn't she? Wait a minute . . .' His voice had changed. He sounded nervous, and I guess if he could have turned any paler, the colour would have drained from his face. 'You're not here as a test, are you?' He glared at me. 'Where is she? Where's the old witch? You can't scare me any more, Mother!' he shouted. 'You can't do any worse to me!'

'There's no one else here,' I said. 'I came on my own.' The statue fell silent and I wondered if I was imagining this whole ridiculous situation; if I'd gone as crazy as everyone else here. I had to get a grip. But then he started up again.

'Okey-dokey. Looks like you are telling the truth. She would've shown herself by now. Open the box, won't you?' he asked. 'Need to stretch my legs.'

I did as he asked, and sure enough the rest of his body was inside. He manoeuvred himself carefully from the box, shedding powder from his rigid joints.

'Who are you, then? What brings you to my humble abode? Don't get me wrong, I'm very glad you came and got me talking and moving again, but what are you doing here?'

'I heard you'd tried to leave the circus, and I thought you might be able to help me to get out of this place.'

'You haven't been here long, have you?' he snorted. 'You can't get out. I tried, and look what happened to me. That was my crime, wanting to go home, so she froze me into a salt fossil.'

'Mother Matushka did this to you?' I gasped. 'She can do that?'

I felt totally sickened, disgusted that she was cruel enough to do this to a boy, not to mention freaked out that it was even *possible*. I was also terrified she'd do the same to me. I'd hardly made a secret of wanting to go home.

'I was even prepared to go *through*. Anything to get away. That's how frantic I was. I would have taken *that* over staying here. Couldn't stand it a second longer. Too many show-offs for my liking. It's like we're all sideshow freaks. Anyway, she said she'd let me go, so she let me through the fire, but then changed her mind and pulled me from the flames. I was burned back to my bones, but here I am, alive as can be – in a manner of speaking. I mean, she can burn us, freeze us and turn us to salt, but not even she can kill what's already dead.'

Dead. The word thudded through me, driving all the crazy pieces into place with the weight of a clunky mallet. *She can't kill what's already dead*. That was it. This boy had been burned alive. Coco claimed to have drowned about a hundred years ago, and Scarlet had survived a knife stabbing right into her neck, and said she'd been to an event that had happened about fifty years ago, when she was nowhere near old enough. No one here needed to eat or sleep, and Mother Matushka had said something about her work being a balancing act between life and death. And I'd seen a headstone with my name on it, and . . . and *everything*. Was everyone here dead? Was this secret circus where the dead go? *Could* they be dead? Was *I*? Had I died and gone to the circus? I might have laughed if I hadn't felt like throwing up. No, this was crazy. It couldn't be true.

'Are you saying . . .?' I asked, eventually. 'Are you saying that everyone here is . . . *dead*?'

But before he could answer, the slap of wet feet sounded behind us. The boy froze, and so did I.

Chapter Sixteen

The slaps stopped right behind me and I felt claws digging into my arms and Mother Matushka's hot, earthy breath burning into my neck. 'So, child,' she said, 'you have learned about my world.'

I turned to face her, not caring that her teeth were clacking like they wanted to bite me, and coils of hair were flailing around her head like snakes preparing to attack. I only cared about knowing the truth, however sick it made me feel, however crazy it was.

'Am I right?' I asked. 'Is it true?'

She went to the boy and examined him and the box, running her hands over his head and the glass. 'Can it be true that you have released this boy from the salt? This is your blood,' she said, rubbing two fingertips together like she was breaking bread into crumbs. 'Your blood in the salt liberated him.'

'Blood?' said the boy. 'She has blood? I thought there was something funny about her. I mean, I thought only you would have been able to make me move again. So what's she doing here, then? And what will happen to me? I mean, what will her blood do to me?'

'Silence!' shrieked Mother Matushka. 'You should think yourself blessed,' she said. 'Blessed by living blood. She made you move, didn't she?'

I couldn't take this any longer. 'Are you going to answer me? Is everyone here . . . are you all *dead*?'

Mother Matushka fixed her eagle eyes on me. 'So, you know what my circus is, you know what we do?' Her voice crackled like leaves on a bonfire. 'I shall speak of who I am, and I shall speak of this place, child. I am Mother Matushka, Mother of Mothers, and in this place everything is my child, and I am everything's Mother. Since the beginning, since the marsh and the mist, I have protected the world of the living from the world of the dead, and the world of the dead from the world of the living. I keep them apart to keep order. And this place, and everything in it, exists *between* the place of the living and the place of the dead.'

'So the people here *aren't* dead?' My head was bursting. 'I don't understand what you're saying.'

'You are not listening, child. The people here are not exactly alive, but neither are they dead. I told you, this is a place of the in-between. The dead pass through the fire in my hearth to their peace, but those who die on thresholds, in in-between places, or in-between states, remain in this place between life and death, and they work with me to keep the boundary sealed.'

Crap. Coco said that she and Lola had died *between* the sea and the sky, and between the water and earth. Did those poor little girls really go through everything Coco had described? And what had happened to everyone else,

140

to Fabian and Accordienka, and Scarlet? *And what about me?* I wondered. Nothing like that had happened to me, so why had I ended up here? And hadn't Mother Matushka just said my blood was living?

'But I can't be . . . I mean, why am I here? I'm not . . .'

'Dead?' She said it for me. 'You arrived on the carousel, as all the dead do, and you were escorted by my horses, as is always the way. But your passage here wasn't as it should be, and it wasn't the time. There hadn't been enough suns and moons since the previous passing. Also, you bleed, you feel hunger. So no, child, you are not dead.'

I caught my breath, partly relieved but still reeling. 'So what am I doing here?'

'That is still a mystery to me. To begin with, I thought you had come to take over my world. To begin with, I thought my struggle with the sun, and the birds obeying you, was because you had broken through to take my place, in the way that the old are replaced by the young in the world you came from. But that's not it, is it? You didn't intend to be here, did you? Lola said you almost drowned in the marsh. You didn't mean to make it shrink, did you?'

'That's what I've been telling –' But she wasn't listening.

'So, while I believe that this disruption is due to you being alive in this in-between place, I do *not* believe it was your intention to cause it. Indeed, I have seen you make harmony here, as well as disruption. You saved me from my own birds; it was in your company that Accordienka found her voice; and you helped me seal my hearth with salt.'

Oh, God. The hearth! My blood ran cold as I suddenly remembered what had happened to me *after* I'd found Granny's letter. It was pouring back to me so fast I felt out of control. The floor around the hearth had collapsed, hadn't it? And I'd fallen through, and just kept falling and falling. And then I remembered that dream I kept having, where I'd seen Mum, Dad and Daisy in that strange room. I couldn't feel my body, and they couldn't hear me, but I could hear them – Daisy blaming Granny, and Mum blaming herself, and saying she knew about Granny being married before. She actually *knew* and hadn't said anything. I remembered the white walls, the overpowering smell, the curtain being drawn . . . What if it hadn't been a dream at all? I blurted this all out, not sure if I was making any sense, but I just had to get it out.

'I had an accident in a hearth,' I said. 'Where my granny died. I fell through it. I hit my head. I think I was in hospital, but it's like I fell through to this world. That must be why I'm here. Maybe I nearly died in that hearth.'

Mother Matushka nodded, slow and sure. No flailing coils, no snapping teeth. She was calm as anything. 'There is no place closer to death than a hearth,' she said. 'It must have claimed you. And now you are here, we shall make good use of you.'

'No.' I panicked. If I wasn't like them, if it had been an accident, I had to be able to go home. 'I shouldn't be here, it was a mistake. There must be a way to leave. I can't stay.'

'Most people see being here as a privilege.' She sounded offended. 'For isn't this another chance to live, and in a most

142

remarkable place, with most remarkable people? A world in which you can do anything you want.'

'Anything *except* what I want,' I said. 'Except going home.'

'I didn't have to invite you to join the others, girl, and I don't have to accept you here. I could destroy you.'

That might have been true, but I sensed that something had shifted. If my blood really had made the boy move, and if my being here was having such an effect on how this world worked, surely I wasn't completely powerless myself?

'Maybe I could do the same to this place,' I said. 'Maybe I could destroy it. Isn't that what's already happening?'

Her crumpled, cagey expression told me I was right.

'I shall be honest with you, there is one way to leave. This boy here, Freddie, had a chance to do so.'

My heart jumped and I opened my mouth to speak, but she waved a finger and went on.

'Freddie has never got used to the idea of having died, and has never settled here. He tried to leave himself at first, several times, but of course the mists kept him in, and the carousel always brought him back, yet still he would not settle, still he wanted no part in what we did here. So I gave him a choice. He could stay and take up his role with the others, or he could go through the blazing hearth with the dead. If he went through and was able to bring me back something I lacked, something I didn't have and could make good use of, I would grant his wish to go home. That way, the balance is kept. I'd have something new, so I'd then be able to let something leave. Freddie weighed up the risks and chose to go through, but when it came to it, I couldn't let him go. I knew he would fail, you see. He talks a lot, but he is not a strong boy. See how he's silent now? You would not have come back, would you, little Fred? You would have been trapped there. Better to be frozen in this cave for a while to make you think, than be burned in the fire and trapped with the dead.'

There was genuine tenderness in the way Mother Matushka spoke about Freddie and, for a split second, everything else left my head. She sounded like she really had kept him in the circus for his own good. I looked at Freddie and just wanted to hug him, because he'd tried to go through, and because Mother Matushka had decided he was too weak for the task, because he *was* too weak for the task. But most of all I wanted to hug him because he was simply a cheeky little boy who'd died far too young and just wanted to go home. But I had to shake myself out of it and concentrate on getting *me* out. While this task might have been beyond Freddie, maybe it wasn't beyond me. However mad or deluded it was, I had to hope; I had to try.

'When can I go?' I asked.

'This passage to the dead can only happen when the next arrivals come, when the hearth is unsealed for them to pass through. There are four more suns before that time. You have four suns to decide.'

That didn't sound long, which I supposed was better than having to wait for ages worrying about it, but that also didn't give me much time to prepare. Although I wasn't sure how you could prepare for doing something like that.

'What's through there? What shall I bring back? I'll do anything you want. I just want to go home to my family.'

'This is your decision to make, but since I am nothing but fair, I will warn you that I have need of nothing.'

'Nothing? Then how is that fair? How could anyone succeed?'

'It is a fair challenge for the magnitude of the reward, child. The dangers of fulfilling it are great. Also, I am being fair in warning you how difficult it is, and I am being fair in strongly suggesting you stay and make the best of things here.' She coughed, throatily. 'I shall leave you to think it over. I must prepare to bring up the sun.' She took hold of Freddie. 'Back to the circus for you, boy. It's time you tried to find your place here again. I haven't given up on you.' She turned back from the brink of the waterfall to face me. '*You* could have a place here, you know. You *have* a place here. We might work well together – as we did with the birds, as you have done with this boy.'

As soon as I was alone, I dropped to the cold ground and bawled like a baby. I thought I would never stop. I made my eyes sore and my throat burn and my head throb. What was I supposed to do? To leave, I'd have to go through a burning hearth with dead people – *dead* people – and somehow find something Mother Matushka didn't have and needed, when she didn't actually need anything. It sounded like a wind-up. Utterly impossible. Then I started wondering what they'd look like. Would they look like people? Zombies from a film? Wispy cartoon ghosts? That's kind of what Coco had said. She'd said something about me not being a shadow, and seeming like a real girl. I understood what she meant now – some of it, at least. I was real, because I was alive, and they weren't. All this time, I'd been going on about finding a way home, and all this time I'd been trapped in a circus of half-dead people. I couldn't stand being left alone in that cave any longer, so I went outside.

The sharp slice of moon was still there, and I wondered if this was the same moon people could see in the real world – if Mum, Dad and Daisy could see this same silver blade. I had to try, didn't I? I couldn't let fear stop me. I guess this was like the biggest audition of all, and if I didn't go through with it, I'd be stuck here forever and I'd never see them again. I thought of them standing over me in that white room. Did they think I was going to die? It was cutting me up to think that Daisy blamed Granny for what had happened, and I was desperate to ask Mum why she'd never said anything. I had to get back to them. I had to try to go through, didn't I? How *could* I have a place here?

Part Three

By the time Vasilisa neared home, the sun had risen and she had no need of the skull's light. But as she went to throw it away, a voice came from it. 'Don't discard me,' it said. 'Take me to your stepmother.' Vasilisa looked at the house and saw it was still dark, so she did as the skull asked and brought it inside.

While Vasilisa had been away, no flame had lit for the stepmother or stepsisters and every flame brought to them by their neighbours had gone out the moment it came into the house, so when she went inside with the light they treated her kindly for the very first time.

'Perhaps your light will last,' said the stepmother. And she was right, for the skull's glowing eyes stared at both her and the stepsisters throughout the night. They were unable to escape its scorching glare and by morning they were burned to ashes, and only Vasilisa was spared.

When the sun rose, she dug a deep hole and buried the skull and walked into town, hoping to find her father. An old, childless woman offered her shelter until her father returned. To keep herself busy while she waited, Vasilisa asked the old woman for some flax and she spent her days spinning. She spun fast as lightning and her thread was as fine as strands of hair, and in no time at all she'd spun a great bundle of yarn. It was too fine to comb and too fine to weave, so she asked her doll for help. Using a comb, a shuttle and the mane of a horse, the doll made a loom and Vasilisa was able to weave the thread herself.

By the end of winter all the thread had been woven and Vasilisa said the old woman could sell the cloth and keep the money, to thank her for giving her shelter. The old woman looked at the cloth and thought it was so fine that only the Tsar himself could wear it, so she took it to the palace and the Tsar was so impressed he gave her great gifts in exchange for it.

Once the old woman had gone, the Tsar ordered new shirts to be made from the cloth, but it was too fine for any of his seamstresses to work with. So he summoned the old woman back and asked her to make them, thinking she'd spun the cloth. When she explained it was the work of a young girl she'd taken in, the Tsar asked for that girl to make them.

The old woman hurried home and told Vasilisa.

'I knew one day I would have to do my own work,' she replied, and she locked herself away and sewed without rest until a dozen shirts were ready.

When the old woman took them to the Tsar, he was so impressed that he wanted to meet the young seamstress for himself. He rode to the cottage and as soon as he saw Vasilisa, he fell in love and asked for her hand in marriage.

And though she was now able to look after herself, and do her own work, Vasilisa carried her doll in her pocket for the rest of her life, to remind her of her mother, and of the time in her life when she needed help.

Chapter Seventeen

Time seemed to stop while I sat there outside the cave. I felt as frozen as Freddie had looked, but not from anything Mother Matushka had done to me, or even the cold. It was like my whole *self* had frozen. All my thoughts, everything I'd ever done, and everything I might have done. Everything had stopped, including my future. I was locked in limbo, until Fabian came. I didn't hear him. He just appeared before me, pulled me to my feet and wrapped me in his arms. And then, finally, I breathed again. I went limp with relief. Not because anything had changed about my situation. It was just overwhelming relief at him being there, at not being totally alone.

'I know, I know,' he said. 'You feel lost now, little Rose, but the shock will pass and you'll feel found again. I know it.'

I'd never been so grateful for company or a hug, but still, part of me was hurt – and angry – that he hadn't told me the truth.

'Why didn't you tell me what this place really is, what you really are? Why did no one tell me?'

'You were an outsider,' he explained. 'You came on your

own, outside the ordinary cycle of things. We supposed you were a danger.'

'A danger?' I almost snorted. I still couldn't really grasp how someone like me could be seen as dangerous. 'I don't know about that, but I *was* on my own. I *am* on my own.'

'I understand. We all feel like that at first, but you will settle in and come to realise how fortunate you are to have another life. A *different* kind of life,' he corrected himself. 'We get to be here, to have all this.' He gestured in the direction of the Big Top.

'Not everyone,' I said. 'Not Freddie. He didn't ever settle in, did he? And I won't either. I don't want this.'

'Let's walk,' he said, softly.

He held out his hand and led me over the bank to the lake. We sat at the edge of the water, watching the moon and its reflection.

'It seems like a tiny thing, but this has always done me good,' he said, his voice barely there.

'What has?' I whispered too. It felt wrong to spoil the peace.

'Drinking in the moon here. It always makes me feel close to the world we came from.'

His words turned my heart. 'I was thinking something like that before you came,' I said. 'It sounds daft, but I was wondering if it was the same moon.'

'I believe it is; I believe they can see it.' He closed his eyes and I saw his lips move, like he was saying a silent prayer. 'I did the same before I came to the circus. Whenever I was apart from my family, I would take comfort from knowing that we could be linked by watching this same moon at the same time, that we were connected by something so much greater than the physical space between us.'

I completely got what Fabian meant, and I also got that he didn't just mean the moon. I mean, it's comforting and romantic to imagine that the people you love are seeing the same incredible thing as you when you're not with them, but more than that, *greater* than that, there's the way people you love are always with you, even when you're apart, because they're part of you. I'd learned that when Granny had gone.

'Did you ever think about trying to leave the circus?' I asked. 'To go home to the people you left behind?'

'I think about them all the time, but I taught myself, early on, not to torture myself with thoughts of leaving.' He sighed, long and deep. 'I have Accordienka. Pining for our past would be harmful to us both, as it is to you, Rosie. It will only prolong your pain.'

Again, I totally understood what he was saying, but I wasn't like him. I felt bad for saying it, but I needed people to stop trying to persuade me I'd be OK here. I wasn't staying.

'I'm different. I'm not supposed to be here.'

'I know you are not like us, but you can work with Mother and play a very important part in what we do here. And you know there's no way back,' he added. 'Being special doesn't change that.'

'I'm not special. Not really. It's all because of a stupid accident.' I skimmed a stone across the lake. The ripples ruined its smoothness. 'And I mean it about trying to get home. Mother Matushka said there's a way. She said if I go through and bring something back she doesn't have, she could give me what I wanted, so I could go home . . .'

I shut up. The edgy look on Fabian's face was scaring me. 'What is it?'

'I must be honest with you.' He took hold of my hands. 'The chances of you succeeding are extremely slight. No one has ever done it. I fear you won't make it back, that you'll be trapped beyond the hearth forever. And there is something else to consider too – your family. You've left that world. Won't they think you've gone, that you've passed on? Even if you do the impossible and return, it cannot bring them any good. Think of them.'

I wasn't sure about that – how could I be? I didn't know how bad I was back there, how close to death I was. Maybe I'd died there since me seeing them in that room. Maybe that's why the curtains had been closed. I felt like I'd slipped through a crack in the world. Could they ever know where I was?

'Does *anyone* know about this place?' I asked. 'Or is it really unseen to everyone outside?'

'To be honest, I've always thought that some people in the world back there knew something – the mythmakers and storytellers, the old soothsayers and wise women who passed on stories about how the world came to be, what happens when we die, and so on. But it wasn't until coming here that I understood the true meaning of those tales.'

I could feel my face flushing. He sounded like Granny. 'Like what?' I asked.

'Like that the witch isn't all bad. She isn't all about death and destruction. While Mother facilitates the passage of

154

the dead, she also protects *life* by upholding this threshold between the two worlds.'

Threshold. There was that word again. Mother Matushka had used it, but I'd come across it somewhere else too. I could see it now, in Granny's spindly writing, in *that* note. Could she have known *this* truth? I might have been reading far too much into this, but it seemed to me now that anything could be true.

'This is going to sound weird,' I said, 'but my granny used to say stuff about tales telling truths. She used to tell me the story about Mashenka and the bear – the one Jacques mentioned – and she told me about Lady Snowstorm. But the thing about thresholds is that after she died I found a letter from her. It was her suicide note.' I swallowed hard. The word choked me. 'I found it in her hearth, close to where she was found. And . . . and it said something about it being time for her to cross the threshold. I had my accident just after reading it. I fell through that same hearth and ended up here. It's too much of a coincidence, don't you think? I can't quite fit all the pieces together, but do you think she *could* have known about this place?'

'That I cannot say, Rosie. I don't know her. It might have been a figure of speech. Death is often referred to as a crossing or passing. Perhaps we all know about the threshold, deep down, just not necessarily in a literal sense. She meant a lot to you, didn't she?'

As I went to reply, Scarlet's sing-song voice rang out. 'Where are you, Fabian? Did you find her?'

'We're down here! By the water,' he called.

She appeared at the top of the bank and waved wildly before bounding down to us.

'Hope you're doing OK, sweetheart. Knew you were special first time I set my eyes on you, but *alive*? That's something else!'

'And you're . . .' I trailed off. It felt rude to actually say the word and also, as I looked at her, all vibrant and healthy-looking, it really hit me how crazy it was that she wasn't actually alive. I'd been so wrapped up in myself I hadn't thought to ask what it was like being them. 'What does it feel like?' I asked. 'To be . . . not alive?'

She held out her arm. 'Touch me,' she said. I put my hand on her wrist. There was no pulse. 'It's like my blood froze the day I died,' she said. 'It's tricky to describe what it feels like from the inside. I guess . . . I guess it's like going to sleep as normal and waking up as a feistier, more fearless version of yourself. As your gutsier twin, or your sassier big sister. It's like when something real bad has happened to you, and you're at that scary, exciting stage of starting to pick yourself up and throw yourself back into the world, open to discovering what new things you can do, what new paths you could take. It's like all those in-between parts of your life, when anything seems possible.'

Her description reminded me of the amazing adrenaline rush I'd felt at a couple of auditions, when everything was flowing and the world was right onside, but you're teetering on the edge because you know you've got to keep it all going and not slip up.

'And on top of that,' she smiled, 'I'll never get any more

wrinkly. I came here in 1957 when I'd just turned thirty. Haven't aged a day since.'

'So, that makes you . . . eighty-six? Eighty-seven? That's crazy. So you meant it when you said you went to that film premiere? You really were there?'

'Sure was, honey. Not bad-looking for such an old broad, wouldn't you say?'

'Not bad at all.' I smiled. 'Do you mind if I ask you something else? Why are you here? I mean, I know about Coco and Lola and the boat accident, but what happened to you?'

'Remember me mentioning that baby I had in my belly? Well, I never got to be her mother.'

Her story really tore at my heart. She'd gone into labour early and died giving birth while her sailor sweetheart was at sea. She'd died on the threshold of motherhood, which was why she'd stayed in the circus.

'I remember the doctors in white masks and the river of blood, and then more red and white – the carousel and the Big Top. And that was that.' She ran a hand over her tattoo. 'Me and my Jack had it all mapped out. That baby was going to turn our lives around. I was going to quit the travelling troupe and find more regular work with a theatre. Of course, I can't know for sure, but I've always felt that she did pull through and made a real good life for herself. I don't even know if she was a girl, but she'll always be my little Martha.'

Scarlet's voice cracked and I went to put an arm round her, but she waved me away. 'Bet she turned out to be a brilliant dancer, what with the way she kept me awake with all her kicking. She'd have been born for the circus.'

That was something else that hadn't occurred to me in all the madness. 'If you all came here from different kinds of lives, why *is* this a circus?'

Scarlet stood up, smiling, and hugged her shoulders. 'See, the thing about circuses, especially ours, is that they contain the whole world, but in glorious Technicolor! In a circus, everything is brighter, more intense, at its extreme. The biggest, the highest, the strongest, the smallest, the fastest. Get it? Everything is here, and everything is exaggerated. You've seen it, haven't you? You saw me on that wheel, and Fab with the fire, and the boys on the wire, and Coco soaring from the ceiling. We can't die, so we can do all kinds of daredevil things. Doesn't matter if you never did anything adventurous before coming here. Doesn't matter if you've never performed. Take Fab, for instance. He came here as plain old Fabianski, a humble country carpenter. Well, not so plain, I guess.' She pinched his cheek, and he smiled in return. 'I mean, you were no performer when you came here, were you, Fab? You *learned* how to be fabulous.'

'You're quite right, Scarlet.' He smiled. 'We can be everything and anything here, because we are neither one thing nor another.'

Scarlet pulled me to my feet and swung me around. 'No constraints, total freedom!' she yelled. 'And you could have that too!'

I hugged her so hard my arms hurt. I felt excited.

I actually felt excited. Right at that moment I wasn't thinking about going home, or what I had to do to get there. I just felt rollercoaster-touching-down-in-a-new-country excited. Heart-in-my-mouth and stomach-in-my-head excited. Mad-crazy excited.

Chapter Eighteen

Scarlet and I were still spinning around when a painfully shrill sound cut right into my ears. I raised my hands to protect them, it was that loud and penetrating.

'Shoot!' Scarlet cursed. 'Sorry, sugar, I was supposed to bring you back to the Place of the Players. Mother wanted your help with the light. She must've sent them.'

She meant Mother Matushka's wolf cubs. They were on the edge of the bank, their relentless yelps and whines on the verge of erupting into full-on howls.

'Do I have to?' I really didn't want to leave. Spending this time with Fabian and Scarlet had been the closest I'd come to feeling at home here.

'She needs you, Rosie, which means we all do, and I'll be for it if I don't get you there. I'm sorry.'

The wolves were getting more and more wound up, and I didn't want to cause any trouble for Scarlet, so after collecting the skull-post from outside the cave we walked towards the Big Top, with me between the two of them. The wind whipped up and made my dress swirl out and up round my shoulders, and the way the clouds were racing across the moon made it look like there was an eclipse every few seconds.

'Feels like my hair's about to blow off!' Scarlet shouted.

'I wish it would stop,' I replied, struggling to control my dress.

'What's that, sweetie?'

'I said I wish it would stop!'

And it did. As I said it, the wind stopped and the night was still. It was like, I remembered, when the marsh had cleared. I'd said I wanted that to stop and then the slime shrank back and I was safe.

'Wowsers!' Scarlet stared at me, actually goggle-eyed. 'Try it again. Say you wish it was windy. Let's see what happens.'

'No. I don't wish it was windy.' But the truth was, I was terrified I *had* made it stop. I guess it could have been a coincidence, but I didn't want to find out that it wasn't. I didn't want to find out I could do things like that, things people aren't supposed to be able to do. I thought of what Granny had said about not being scared of what I could do, and felt a stab of guilt, but this was too much.

'Why not, honey? This is *exactly* the kind of thing I was talking about. You can do anything.'

'Leave her be, Scarlet,' said Fabian. 'If she does not want to, she does not have to.'

I was grateful Fabian had stepped in so I could carry on pretending I was normal, but when we reached the Place of the Players there was nowhere to hide, and I just wanted to bolt back to the cave. There were hundreds of them, maybe thousands, watching me, with the shadows of flames dancing on their masks and painted faces and animal heads. And this time I knew what they were. *Half-dead people.*

It was unnervingly silent. There was no music, no talking. It was like they were waiting for something, and I knew that something was me. Scarlet must have sensed my urge to run, because she squeezed my hand and nudged me forward.

'Don't be scared, honey,' she said. 'Be excited, be strong. Think of it like you went to sleep and woke up princess of the world's most amazing kingdom.'

But that wasn't at all what I felt like. I felt small and awkward as I walked through them towards Mother Matushka. She looked different – smaller, somehow even more swathed by fur, like she was being eaten by her cloak.

'What am I supposed to do?' I asked her.

'We must move down the moon and make the sun come. If we cannot, this place will stay in the half-light, and the days will not pass, the Riders won't respond, and the newcomers won't come.' Her voice was a gravelly half-whisper. I don't suppose she wanted everyone to hear how out of control things were.

'Can't anyone else help?' I asked. 'I mean, Fabian is much stronger than me, and so is Scarlet.'

'I have asked you,' she said. 'I've seen you do things they can't. It is not very different from when you captured the birds and controlled them. Do you remember that?' I nodded. Somehow, I *had* managed to calm them. At least, that's what it had looked like, and I'd felt something too – that invisible thread between me and them. 'Come,' she said. 'Let's go higher. Let's move closer to the sky. Follow my steps and follow my actions.'

We walked through the trees and started to climb the verge that lay beyond them. She moved up over the rocks, swift and sure as a lizard, but her chest rattled and wheezed like a broken squeezebox. I just about managed to keep up with her, scraping my knees and knuckles on the sharp rocks as I clambered behind. It wasn't until we'd almost reached the top that I glanced over my shoulder and registered how high we'd climbed, and how dangerous it was. *Don't look down, don't look back. Don't look down, don't look back*, I chanted to myself, over and over, but I couldn't move another step.

'I can't,' I said. 'I'm stuck. I can't do it.'

Mother Matushka held out her hand. I didn't believe she could take my weight, but her tug was firm and her arms felt as strong as cables and she pulled me to safety.

'Open your eyes,' she said. 'You are safe. Look at our world.'

The Big Top, ringed by flames, and then the forest, and the lake, looking like a mirror with the moon hanging over it, was the most incredible view I'd ever seen. Truly breathtaking.

'A thing of beauty, yes?' she said. 'But we have work to do. Let us draw down the moon and raise up the light for the worlds to keep moving.' She aligned herself with the circus tent, with the moon and the lake on her right, and stretched out her arms. 'Join me, child. Since the time of the marsh and mists I have raised the sun to bring warmth and light, to keep things revolving. Now, it seems, I cannot do it alone. I need you to try with me, child. I insist you try.'

'What must I do?'

'You must do as I do, child, and you must think. You must think and feel. Feel that the sun is in your skin and in your bones. And when your hands feel the wheel on which the sun and the moon revolve, we must press to the right.'

Copying her, I stretched out my arms and clenched my hands. Then I closed my eyes and thought about the sun and the light and all those things she'd said, and I felt an incredible force in my hands, like I really was holding an invisible wheel. My arms were taut and trembling from gripping it so hard.

'Push everything into it, child,' said Mother Matushka, and there was urgency in her voice. 'Press down the moon.'

As I pushed harder and harder, something snapped and I lost my grip. The moon had shifted down, it was now dipping into the lake. On the other side, to our left, the sun was a thin curve peeking above the horizon. The light was like nothing I'd seen. The sky above was still pitch black, but on the side of the moon it was purple and orange with wisps of pink, and on the side of the sun it was yellow and white, also with wisps of pink.

'Take hold again,' she said. 'It can't be left like this. We can't leave them wedged in limbo, stuck halfway like this.'

We strained again, and I felt another snap.

'Have we done it?' I asked, catching my breath. The moon was no longer visible, but the sun still hadn't fully risen. I could see more of it now, but still only a hazy half-globe. 'Will it come up by itself?'

'It will not, but I cannot do any more. Not now, not yet. I have nothing left.' She was wheezing.

'I could keep trying. I'm not tired yet.' I was sweating from all the effort, but still buzzing with energy.

'No,' she said. 'We shall try later, back at the cottage when I've recovered.'

I started to follow her down the rocks, but I couldn't go – I couldn't give up – so I scrambled back up and repositioned myself. This time, when I found the wheel, I pushed even harder into the pressure. Suddenly, my arms shot down and, through my closed eyes, I sensed a change in the light. I opened them and saw that the sun was now a full, bright, orange sphere, and the circus was bathed in its rays.

I'd made the sun rise.

Had I made the sun rise?

From further down the cliff, Mother Matushka replied as if I'd said this aloud. 'Yes, child. You have made the sun rise, and you revived the boy I froze. You can do my work, for which I thank you, and you can undo my work, about which I am uncertain.'

Her voice was faint, and she looked terribly sad, which made me feel guilty. I mean, I knew I hadn't deliberately made Freddie move again, and I knew she'd asked me to help her with the sun, but I felt bad she hadn't been able to do it herself. She said nothing more as we descended the rocks and returned to the Place of the Players. She said nothing until they fell silent, and then she addressed them.

'This child from outside has brought life to this place of half-death. Our Circus of the Unseen has been seen,' she said. 'Our world has been changed, and we cannot go back to the way we were.'

'Why not?' It was Lola, never afraid to speak out. 'This is our place, not hers. She's not meant to be here, is she? She's not like us. She shouldn't change anything. She shouldn't be doing the sun.'

'Once something has changed, Lola, once things have moved on, they never go back to how they were. Is your life here as it was before you arrived? Was your life on the island the same as it was in England? Are your mind and your heart as they were before those experiences?'

Lola shook her head, and I knew Mother Matushka was right too. I knew you couldn't stop things from changing, and I knew you couldn't turn things back, no matter how much you wished something hadn't happened.

'She shall work alongside me,' Mother continued. 'She shall be welcomed into all that we do, for as long as she's here.'

Those words sent a shudder through me. Me raising that sun meant I was a day closer to having to make a decision. Time was edging towards my chance to go home, towards me having to attempt the impossible. I didn't notice Mother Matushka leave. I stood there in a daze, thinking about what had just happened, and what she'd said about things changing and not being able to go back to how they were. And I was thinking about Granny dying, and how that had changed us all, and I wondered how me not being at home had already changed Mum, Dad and Daisy.

All this was whirling round in my head when I noticed that the music had started up, and it sounded just like the inside of my head – an out-of-control, jumbled mess. I caught

Scarlet's eye. She was with Fabian, just outside the Big Top, on her horse, wearing a sequined corset and a tutu that stuck out at her hips. 'Rosie!' she called, waving both arms. I went as close as I could. The creature still looked calm as anything, but then so had the one that ran off with Granny.

'Fancy a ride on Sunny Blaze? I could teach you to twirl on her, if you like. You seem light on your feet. I mean, the way you went up those rocks was amazingly brave, not to mention the little matter of you raising the sun.' She arched an eyebrow, grinning from ear to ear. 'What did I tell you? Wasn't I right?'

'I was just helping.' I shrugged. 'Mother Matushka told me what to do.' It wasn't like I'd worked really hard and become good at something. It was just a weird consequence of me being here, which was a horrible, freakish accident. 'And I'm not sure about riding. I'm not keen on horses.'

'You can bring people to life and you can raise the sun, but you're scared of horses? How about the trapeze, then? You gotta try something. Just you, me and the Fabulous Fabianski, with no one else watching. Reckon you have the poise for it.'

Scarlet's encouragement must've really got under my skin because I found myself saying yes, I would like to try the trapeze, as long as it was just the three of us. And she had a point about climbing those rocks. I'd managed to hold it together up there. OK, I'd frozen near the summit, but I hadn't totally crumbled. I'd climbed back and finished the job on my own. That had been much more dangerous than being stuck up a tree, scared of a snake that was actually a worm. It was also braver than getting back on a stage after that disastrous audition. And I'd actually done it.

Scarlet flipped back the opening to the Big Top, and I could see there was no one there, so I went inside determined to keep going, desperate to try more, without anyone being there to see any mistakes I might make.

'You should wear something more showy, Rosie,' Scarlet suggested. 'Pick something from that chest. Maybe one of the little ribbon dresses.'

'You mean this?' It was hardly a dress at all, though she was right about it being little. It had a tight red bodice and a skirt made of red and white ribbons, like a maypole.

Once I'd changed, Scarlet scaled up a pole to a swing. She tossed down a harness to Fabian and he fixed it around my waist. Before I had a chance to psych myself up, I was already being hoisted up into the air. I screwed my eyes shut, feeling queasy from all the swinging and the thought of there being nothing but a thin wire stopping me from smashing onto the sawdust below.

'Grab the swing, sweetie!' Scarlet hollered. I opened my eyes and reached out for it but kept snatching at air, missing it by milliseconds. After a few attempts, though, I managed to grab hold of it with the tips of my fingers. Once it was in my grasp, and while she was swaying back and forth on her own giant pendulum, Scarlet somehow managed to help me manoeuvre myself into a sitting position. 'Loosen up, let yourself go,' she said. 'I know that's against instinct, but that's the trick. Go with it, don't fight it.'

Finger by finger, I relaxed my grip. I was still holding tight, but less tensely, and I found myself easing into the rhythm of soaring from one side of the ring to the other. The more I relaxed, the more I actually enjoyed it, until I noticed other people coming inside. Now the space was no longer just ours, I tensed up again and slipped off the swing, ending up dangling from the harness, floppy and uncoordinated as a ragdoll. Fabian caught hold of my legs and slowed me down until I was back on the ground with my blood still pumping like crazy.

'You did well, Rosie,' he said, unharnessing me. 'Very well for your first attempt. What do you think, Lola?' he called. She was standing close by, staring at me with narrowed eyes. 'You know about the swings.'

Lola shrugged, but coming from her a shrug made me feel like I'd been paid the world's biggest compliment. Now I knew what had happened to her and Coco, I didn't blame her for being so hostile. Of course I didn't. She had to look out for her sister, didn't she? She'd had to become a parent to her little sister, and no one could blame her for being protective after being bullied in one country and made an outcast in another. Their story was one of the most heartbreaking things I'd ever heard, more than I imagined a person could cope with. I went up to her.

'I'm sorry about what brought you here. Coco told me last night.'

'That's none of your business,' she snapped.

'I just wanted to tell you how brave I think you are. I mean, for doing what you did to help your parents.' As I turned away, she caught hold of my arm.

'Wait,' she said. 'Do you mean that?'

'Course. I wouldn't have said it otherwise.'

'It's just that . . . that –' She broke off. 'It wasn't brave at all. It was stupid. It's my fault Coco died.'

'You can't mean that. You mustn't even think it. It was an accident, wasn't it? It wasn't your fault, and you're here together, aren't you? You've given her this new life.'

I realised I sounded like Scarlet, but I was starting to see for myself that they were lucky to be here, and Lola confirmed that.

'It *was* my fault,' she insisted, 'but I do sometimes think it's better for us in the circus than it was in the other world. I'll never forgive myself for what I did to Coco, and for leaving Mother and Father, but people made us leave our homes and called us monsters there. That would never happen here.' She looked at her feet for a moment, then caught my eye. 'I'm sorry I was nasty to you.'

I shook my head and smiled, to tell her it was OK. 'But what about Freddie?' I asked. He was sitting near the edge of the ring with his back to the performance area. 'Why hasn't he fitted in? Why does he still want to leave?'

'Look at him. He never joins in. He never even tries.'

I felt even worse for the poor boy when Lola told me how he'd come to be here. He'd died in his work as a sweep, up a chimney, between fire and air. I went to him and asked if he wanted to try the trapeze with me, or anything he fancied, but he turned on me.

'Do you think I give a damn about the trapeze, girl? Think you're so special, don't you? And now Mother's giving you

171

a chance to go while I'm stuck here. Not my fault I can't do all that stuff with the moon and the sun, is it? Not my fault I died.'

He turned away, and I felt awful for having no words to make him feel better.

'What did I tell you? Just leave him.' Lola touched my arm. 'Do *you* want to try the trapeze again? I can show you how to move less like a dodo.' She raised her eyebrows and grinned.

'You mean because they can't fly? Come on, I didn't think I was that bad. It was my first time, and I'm frightened of heights.' I smiled. 'But, yes, I'd like another go.'

As she strapped me into the harness and I rose up over the ring, I realised it was pretty amazing that only one of all the people down there beneath me hadn't come to feel at home here. But that wasn't any help to Freddie. I really wanted to find some way to help him feel at home. Before I knew it, I was swinging like crazy again. Lola tried to persuade me to let go and swap swings with her midflight, but there was no way I could do that yet. I did hang from the bar by one hand, though, and when we finished she told me I still moved like a dodo but one that was trying to be a swan, which I took as a compliment.

I spent the rest of the day in the Top, watching Scarlet do acrobatics on her horse, and the Fabulous Fabianski juggle with fire, and the Wolf Brothers and Flamingo dancers and Dolly Dimple and everyone else do what they did, until Mother Matushka came and we drew down the sun and drew up the moon, and they lay down to rest. Then I went with her to the cottage and we sealed the hearth with earth and salt and I lay down near the fire. But even though I was exhausted, I couldn't sleep because my head was spinning with the thought that I was a moon closer to having to go through the hearth and leave them.

Chapter Nineteen

I woke up alone. The cottage door was ajar and I could see Mother Matushka's silhouette stretched across the grass, wavering in the skull-light. The wolf cubs were at her feet and there were birds' bodies strewn all over the garden. They were dainty little things, not like the massive crow-like creatures I'd seen here before. Their feathers were as bright as the roses round the door, a dazzling shock of blue. But their wings were bloodied and broken, their beaks shattered. My first thought was that the wolves had run rampage. 'What happened?' I asked Mother Matushka.

'A sign,' she said. 'The death of hope, the end of innocence. But didn't we already know that? Hasn't the wheel of my world already turned? And as one era slips down, so another ascends.' She coughed and spluttered. She looked really ill. Her eyes were dull and sunk deep into her skull. 'I drew them down to their deaths, that's what happened. I was disturbed by a terrible scratching on the roof. When I came outside, they gathered around me, all flapping and fretting, so I drew them down to calm them, but I drew them to their deaths.' She cradled one to her chest. 'They crashed into the earth. All of them broken, all dead, and this is not a place of death. Nothing should die here. This is a place for blossoming.' She closed the bird's eyes and laid it on the ground. 'You are a blossom. I am weak, as old as the earth and the mists and the marsh but, until now, I have never felt it. I have felt the wisdom of age, but not the weakness.'

I didn't know what to say. I felt bad I hadn't heard anything. 'You should have woken me. Maybe I could have helped.'

'I suppose you could, but don't fret, child. It's done with, and now it's time for the sun. I shall drink a drop of rose brew, then do the rising here. I don't have the strength to go to my Top just yet.'

She went inside and I got on with bringing up the sun myself. I couldn't bear to see her struggle again. I did the thinking, the feeling and the taking hold of the wheel well enough, but when it came to the pressing down part, I pushed far too hard and lost control. The light shot from the black of night to the purple of dusk in seconds, with only a flash of daylight sun in between. *Crap*. I heaved it back, like I was steering a huge ship, taking care not to pull too hard or let go too soon. I pulled until I felt it click into place. Then I held my grip steady for several minutes before letting go, scared it might slip away again. I breathed deep when it stayed where it was. Then I laid out all the bodies together in a corner of the garden, thinking this wasn't the first time I'd cleared up dead birds.

As I turned to join Mother inside, I heard something shuffle behind me. One of the birds was moving – fragile and dazed and newly hatched looking, but it was alive.

'Look!' I cupped it in my hands. It was straining to move its beak, too weak to make a sound, but there was movement, there was life.

Mother rushed outside and took the bird from me. She nestled it in the sleeve of her cloak and brought it inside. 'One survivor,' she said. 'Or was it you?' she asked me. 'Did your touch revive it?'

That seemed unlikely, as none of the others were alive and I'd touched them all, but she wasn't waiting for an answer. She was engrossed in tending to the little bird, so I got on with scattering the salt and the earth around the hearth for her.

'That's it, child,' she said. 'Be sure to sweep away any dust. The way must be clean for their passing, and for the fresh dolls.'

I swallowed hard. Was I really going to do it? Could I go through with them?

'What exactly are the dolls for?' I asked. 'Did you say they were called soul sisters, or something?'

'Soul Mothers, that's what they are,' she explained. 'As the dead pass through the hearth, their souls are captured in the dolls. There is no need of a soul through there, you see. Souls are life, through there is death, and they need to be separated. That is the way of things. That is always the way. There must always be a line.' She traced one in the air, from left to right.

'So,' she said. 'You have made up your mind? Knowing the risks and the unlikelihood of success, you are still fixed on trying to return to your world?'

As I nodded, I realised I didn't know for sure. I didn't know if I could. I didn't know if I should.

'If you *are* still planning to pass through,' she went on, as if she'd sensed my doubt, 'you should join the procession of those who are passing through as they leave the Big Top and make their final journey to cross this threshold.' She gestured at the fireplace.

I shivered as I thought of actually having to do it, but that wasn't the only thing on my mind.

'What will happen to you when I go? Will things go back to how they were before I came and messed things up?'

'Truthfully, I do not know. Perhaps I will be strong again, or perhaps I still won't be able to raise the sun myself. And without that regular cycle, perhaps the carousel won't come, and the dead won't pass. I don't know. It has never happened before. You are a first.'

I felt sick with guilt. I'd done this – not deliberately, obviously, but it was my fault.

'But these matters are mine, not yours, child. As you have said, this is not your world, but it *is* mine.' Mother Matushka looked me in the eye, and even though hers were tired and hollow, I saw a flash of fire in them, and it caught me. I was held in their glare. 'But it is better to do what needs to be done than to wallow in imagining what might come to pass. And what I need to do now is watch over this bird, and I need you to check if Fabian has the new dolls ready.'

The air near the lake was cool and fresh, and the water clean and clear. Everything was calmer and the walking did my head some good, I think. Fabian was outside his hut with a brush in his mouth and green paint streaked in his hair. The dolls were laid out on a workbench in front of him.

'They look amazing,' I said. 'You're a pretty good painter.'

'Thank you, Rosie.' He smiled. 'That's something I learned here. My wife used to paint them. They are almost ready, just a few more to finish decorating. But what happened with the sun just now? I saw the light come up, and then fall dark for a moment. Is everything all right?'

'That was my fault. I moved it too far. Mother was shattered from drawing down the birds. It went wrong, they all crashed into the earth, and we thought they'd all died, but one of them started to move as I cleared them up. Mother's looking after it now. She sent me to see if the dolls are ready.'

I was fighting it, but actually seeing the dolls, all ready for the arrivals, was too much. A tear burst. I watched it drop onto Fabian's hand in extra-slow motion.

'Rosie? What is it?' He put an arm round my shoulder and sat me on the bench, and I spilled how guilty I felt about what I'd done to the circus, and about what might happen if I left, and how awful I felt for even thinking I might stay and pass up a chance to go back to Mum and Dad.

'Slow down, Rosie. Slow down.' He rubbed my back until I caught my breath. 'I can tell you the facts I know. I can tell you I think you are more likely to have a life if you stay. Look at what you're doing here with Mother, and think of how you enjoyed the trapeze.' He smiled a sweet half-smile before his face fell serious again. 'But I can also tell you that if I were you, I might be tempted to try to go home, which I know is no use to you at all. Only you can know what is right for you.' He shook his head. 'I once lost someone very special because they went back to something. I wish I'd begged harder for them to stay. I wish they'd never gone.'

Him saying that made me wish he'd beg *me* to stay. I wish he'd come right out and say it and make my decision for me.

'And then I never saw them again,' he explained. 'I left that world soon after.'

'What happened to you?' I sniffed. 'If you don't mind me asking?'

'It was many decades ago. The war was ending, we were told, but then a bomb hit our village and killed almost everyone. The few of us who survived fled towards the border, where things were supposed to be better. Accordienka was so excited when I pointed out the other country ahead of us that she ran off, into the no-man's-land between the two borders. I went after her, and that's when it happened. We were shot. She was first. She was still holding my hand when she fell to the ground, and as fast as this –' he snapped his fingers, and I jumped – 'she was dead. And the next thing I knew, the last thing I remember, is my eyes filling with blood and the world blacking out in that grey, in-between place.'

'I'm so sorry. But what about your other daughter, and their mum? Where were they?'

'That was the person I should have begged to stay. My wife, their mother. She'd gone back to her own country, to take care of her sick mother. And as for my other daughter, I don't know what happened to her. She went with us towards the border, but she was a little way behind. She wasn't with us when we went into no-man's-land, so perhaps she survived, perhaps she lives on still. All I know is that my little Lilka did not come here with us.'

Lilka. The name sent a bolt right through my heart. *It is time for me to join those I left behind, my Bear and my girls, my Anastazja and Lilka.* That's what Granny's letter had said. I could see her spidery writing now. In that instant, hearing that name, after all the stuff about the war, and a bomb, and a sick mother, made my whole world explode and come together at the same time. I could hardly get the words out.

'Did – did Accordienka have a different name before she came here, before the Circus? Did she used to be called Anastazja, or something?'

'Yes. Did she tell you? She hasn't been called that for many years. Her mother chose the name, and the strange thing is that Anastazja means "reborn", which I suppose is what has happened to her. What is it, Rosie? You look like you've seen a ghost.'

And the thing was, I *had* practically seen a ghost, and she was standing just a few feet away, holding her doll and singing to herself in a language I now knew must be Polish. I took Granny's doll from my pocket and passed it to Fabian.

'Where did you get this?' His brow was all crumpled, and his eyes kept darting from me to the doll. I couldn't tell if he was angry or upset. 'I made this for the girls' mother. There were two sets, three dolls in each. Before she left, my wife gave each of the girls the smallest.'

'And I bet the dolls in the other set had blonde hair and blue shawls, and I bet they have the same words carved underneath as the one you're holding.'

Fabian still wasn't getting it, and who could blame him? It was mad, but now I'd worked it out, I couldn't believe I hadn't realised earlier.

'My grandmother gave me two sets of dolls just before she died, with only two dolls left in each. I put one of mine in her grave, but I kept this one, and my sister has the two blue dolls. Do you know what that means? You're him, aren't you?' I took hold of his arm. 'You're the man she loved, you're her Bear. I know it. I know Granny's girls were called Anastazja and Lilka. I read it with my own eyes.'

Once I'd started I couldn't stop. It was like a river had burst. I just kept thinking of more things that were falling into place and churning up, all at the same time. 'Your wife's name was Dorothy Rose, wasn't it? That's what the "DR" carved into the dolls stands for. Same initials as me. Dorothy Rose is my real name.'

'Yes, that was her name. I called her my Różyczka, my little Rose, and I was her Bear. But how can this be? It *can't* be.'

Fabian's eyes welled up. He ran his fingers through his hair, and I just wanted to tear mine out. I hated seeing him upset like this, but I had to get him to believe me. What more could I say?

'Hang on. Look at this.' I unfastened my necklace and handed it to him. 'She was looking for it just before she died. I found it afterwards, with some letters from you, and some babies' shoes. They must have been your daughters' shoes.'

I thought he was going to pass out when he saw the necklace. He stumbled and collapsed onto the bench.

'I made this for her,' he said, stroking the charm. 'I gave it to her before she went back to England. This is impossible. *Impossible*.'

'What was her favourite dress?' I asked in desperation. 'She was wearing it in a photo taken outside a cabin, by a lake.' As I said it, I realised something else: they'd both recreated their lives with each other; Granny with her cabin next to the house, and Fabian with this hut by the lake.

'I remember that day well. There were not many photos. She wore a yellow ribbon in her hair, and her dress was green, and patterned with dots.'

'*Dots*.' We said it together, then both fell silent for what felt like an age. I pressed my hands to my face, holding my breath, waiting for him to say something. My heart gulped when he did.

'When I first saw you . . . your eyes, they held me, and now I know why. They are like my little Rose's. I saw them sparkle like hers when you flew on the trapeze, and when you raised the sun. And I can see it now. This is truly astonishing, unbelievable. Can it be true?' He took hold of my arm. 'Do you know what happened to Lilka?'

I didn't know how to tell him that Granny had hardly mentioned them. I shook my head. 'She couldn't say much. It upset my mum.'

I'd been thinking about that for a while, ever since I remembered Granny's letter, trying to understand why Mum had never spoken about them. I think I would have wanted to meet my half-sisters, not pretend they didn't exist, but Mum was an only child. Maybe that made it harder to accept you weren't the only special one in your mother's life, especially if Granny still missed them so much. It must have been agony for them both.

'What *did* she say about us?'

'Just before she died she started telling me more about this time in her life, and I could see how much she missed you. I even suggested we visit your village, to see if anyone had survived. After she'd gone and I found your letters and the necklace, I decided I was going to find out everything I could, but then I had my accident –' I broke off, my face burning as it hit me that I must have been right about Granny knowing about this place. And that wasn't all.

'I know this will sound crazy, but I really think she was trying to come to you *here*. She wasn't just trying to die and join you in death. She didn't mean it as a metaphor, or something. She was trying to die *on a threshold* so she'd come to you.'

'What are you saying, Rosie? That she . . . she killed herself to try to come to me?' He looked horrified. 'Are you sure? Even if she knew something about the in-between world, how would she know I was here?'

'Because she knew how you died. She knew that people from your village were killed as they were about to cross a *border*. She told me about a report she'd read. I think she meant to die on the threshold of the hearth. She was found *near* it.' I bit my lip as more pieces of the puzzle fell into place. 'And I don't think that was the first time she'd tried either.'

184

I told him about Granny's riding accident that time we were on holiday in Germany. It seemed likely to me now that she'd ridden that horse into the road deliberately. That had happened on a border.

'My darling little Rose.' He shook his head. 'Maybe she did know something. We shall never know for certain, but I am sure about one thing.' Fabian smiled, and the way his whole face lifted and lit up made tears stream down my cheeks. 'I am sure that it is a wonderful thing that we have found each other. I am more glad than I can ever say.'

As we hugged, I felt excited and weak at the same time. I now knew Granny's secrets, and I'd met the people she'd loved and left behind, and it broke my heart all over again to think of her being that desperate to join Fabian and her girls here. In a way, she'd brought me here. My accident and falling through came about because I was searching for her secrets in the place she'd died. But what now? What was I going to do? I had my answer to that too, and it made me tingle all over.

Suddenly, the air turned colder. I raised my head from Fabian's shoulder. Thick clouds were closing in fast, blocking out the light. Something cold and wet landed on my nose. Snowflakes! Delicate, plump flakes, falling in swirls that were rapidly covering the ground. Didn't that mean it was time? Hadn't Mother Matushka said she shakes out the snow before the horses come, and before *they* come?

'It's snowing,' I hissed. 'Look.'

'The snow? I don't understand. There's still another sun to rise.'

Crap.

'That must be my fault. I moved it too far, didn't I? I had to drag it back, so I suppose it rose twice this morning.'

'I'll go to Mother with the dolls. Will you make sure Scarlet knows?' He took hold of my hand. 'But have you decided, Rosie? You're not leaving us, are you? Don't go through, don't leave us, I beg you.'

Well, I had to stay, didn't I? I had to listen to their warnings about how impossible it was, and I had to say goodbye to Mum, Dad and Daisy. I ached for what I no longer had – for them – but I also felt lighter, knowing I was now free to get on with what I had here.

'If you're begging, I'll stay, *Granddad.*'

'Yes, I suppose I'm *almost* your grandfather. Your impossibly young grandfather!'

He smiled and pressed the necklace into my hand. We hugged again and I ran from the lake through the carpet of snow, imagining that Granny's Lady Snowstorm was shaking her skirts for me.

Chapter Twenty

'Scarlet!' I knocked against her wagon. 'The snow's here! Fabian said I should fetch you.'

I heard her scramble to the door. 'Already? It can't have. Jeez, you're right. I need to get going, I'm not where I'm supposed to be. What's going on?' She ducked back inside and pulled on a cloak. 'Here, have this.' She wrapped a fur stole around my bare shoulders.

'I sort of made the sun rise twice this morning, which is probably why it's early. But I'm not leaving, Scarlet!' I said. 'I'm not going through. I'm staying. I'm definitely staying, if Mother will let me. I haven't had a chance to tell her yet.'

'Of course she'll let you, darling. Look at how you're working with her – although you might want to hold back on raising the sun twice in a day in future. I'm so happy you made the right decision. Have to admit, you had me worried.' She spun me around and squeezed me so hard I could hardly breathe. I wriggled myself free.

'But there's something else,' I said. 'A connection between me and Fabian. We're sort of related. His wife, Accordienka's mum, was my granny. It's incredible, isn't it? I'd already been wondering if – maybe – I should stay, but finding that out made my mind up.'

'What? Seriously? Your grandmother and Fab?' She frowned.

'I know it sounds crazy, but it's true. It really is. There's no doubt.'

'You're *seriously* serious? You're right, that does sound crazy. I need to know all about it, but we really need to get going. I'm afraid you're going to have to take a ride with me on Sunny Blaze, sweetheart. Reckon you can do it?'

I nodded. I had to. Scarlet went round the back of the wagon and returned with the horse. She helped me onto it before jumping up herself, and soon we were pounding through the snow, with me holding tight around her waist.

'We need to go out to the Edge, to the carousel,' Scarlet called. 'Everyone gathers there to greet them and get them to the Top.'

We rode beyond the Big Top and the rocky verge, passing dozens of performers as we went. They were all in costume, and there were more animals than I'd seen before. The tightrope-walking brothers had their wolf heads, the flamingo-costumed girls seemed to have real wings, and there was a brown bear walking on its hind legs. *Was that Fabian?* I wondered. Had he really taught himself to turn into a bear?

We raced ahead of the procession and stopped when we came to the carousel in the clearing. Mother Matushka was there with the bluebird still tucked into her cloak.

'Fabianski tells me you have decided to stay,' she said.

'I welcome you, again, to our world. I hope everyone here will come to feel like your family, not just him and Accordienka.'

'Thank you,' I said. 'Thank you.'

Just then the ground started rumbling and the sky darkened and the carousel music started to ring out. All the performers flooded into the area and rushed towards the noise and the blur of lights that were switching from ruby and gold, to silver and blue, then red and white. Mother Matushka gestured for me to join them, so I ran with blood beating in my eardrums and my feet crunching into the snow. Then everyone stopped and I saw we were no longer under the open sky. There was a wooden cover over us. We were, somehow, on the carousel.

'Hello, Rose Girl.' Coco smiled. She was hovering above me, with no strings attached. 'Look, it's you and Scarlet and Mother Matushka!' she giggled, pointing at the manikin woman.

I had to admit it did look a lot like the three of us, but more than that, maybe, it was like seeing the same woman at different stages of her life. Her three faces blurred into one as the carousel picked up speed.

'When are the new people arriving, Coco?' I asked.

'They're not exactly people, silly! They're more like shadows. Can't you see them? They're here now. They're always here before we come to help them. Look!'

At first I could only see performers I recognised from the circus, but then I noticed that they each had a hazy silhouette behind them, like a shadow that belonged to someone else. Their size and shape revealed their age. Some were hunched and faded, others were small and bright. My eyes were drawn to two that looked different from the others. They had the same fuzzy outline, but they still had bodies, pulsating with silvery light.

As the music faded, I heard the pounding of hooves. A white horse was circling us, and every place it passed became light as dawn. The carousel slowed to a standstill, and I heard the boatman's voice. '*The river don't stop, and the river don't rest,*' he sang, and I realised there was water beneath us. '*The river keeps a-flowing when there's no flesh left.*' Somehow, we were now crossing the lake to the Big Top. When we reached land, Mother Matushka came to me and pulled me aside.

'Stay near me, child. They have a job to do. Yours is to watch what I do. Next time you can partake.'

We went towards the Big Top with everyone following behind. I joined her in the centre of the ring while the others, the Players and their shadows, filed around its edge. A bright, white light shone through the dome of the Top, making it look like the membrane inside an egg. Mother Matushka settled on the ground, and I did the same, while each of the Players took to their wires or cannons, to their diving boards or trapeze swings, to do whatever it was they did. The sound the musicians were making was like nothing I'd ever heard. In it, I heard laughter and pain and anger and love. It was like hearing people's hearts. I could hear Coco and Lola's voices ringing out over everything else, and I could hear Accordienka's drone underpinning everything. It was the root of the music. It was like hearing and feeling the hearts of all the people I had ever known.

'It is time.' Mother Matushka raised her arms and the light shifted and the Big Top was transformed into a great red-and-white cathedral. A Red Rider – it was Scarlet, of course – hurtled into the ring followed by a parade of girls on ponies. The music was frantic now, careering up and down, mad-crazy fast, out of breath and desperate, and the bundle of Mother Matushka next to me twitched, and the smell of salt and earth filled the air. As she stood, all music and movement faded to quiet stillness.

'I had the strength to do it alone,' she whispered, her eyes shining bright. 'I shook the snow, and brought the Riders. I raised the light in the Top.' She turned to me, almost smiling. 'Or was it because you were at my side? Was it both of us?'

I didn't know, but I was glad to see her happy. As we watched the Players leave the Big Top with the shadows at their sides, I felt a twinge in my heart. Mother had said I should join them as they left the Top. This was it. The time had come, but I knew what I had to do. I knew I had to stay and do work here.

By the time Mother Matushka and I came outside, the Players had formed a passageway, with a shadow positioned before each of them. I noticed that the two figures with bodies were standing in line with the Players. They must have died on thresholds, I thought. They must be staying.

Mother and I walked through the passage with the Red Rider following behind, bringing bright daylight in her wake. When we came to the crossroads, Scarlet and Sunny Blaze raced off and crossed paths with the Black Rider that was coming towards us. The switch to darkness was instant. I could no longer see the Players, only the glow of the shadows.

Mother Matushka and I went to the cottage, with the shadows close behind us. She closed the door, took Fabian's new dolls from her cloak, and together we opened them up and stood them on the hearth, ready to be filled. Then she swept away the salt and the earth and unhooked the pot from the fire.

'We are ready,' she said. 'The way is open. When I let them in, you must stand aside so the souls can be gathered in the dolls' bellies. Then we shall put on their heads to seal them inside while the shadows slip through the fire. Once they have passed, we shall reseal the way.'

I took a deep breath as Mother Matushka let them in, and closed the door behind them. The room filled with the shadows' intense white light and, as they moved as one towards the fire, the base of each doll glowed. Once their glow had faded, we closed them up, and the shadows were sucked towards the flames. I'd just closed the very last doll when the door burst open. Freddie rushed across the room.

'What are you doing here, boy?' screeched Mother, scurrying to close the door. 'Get back!' she shouted. 'Stop him, child!'

'I'm going through with them. Can't stand it any more!'

He went to leap into the fire. I grabbed his torso and pulled him back from the flames to safety. He was still kicking like crazy and lashing out at me as I put him down. He sent me reeling backwards towards the hearth. I screamed as the heat licked my arms and legs. I struggled to regain my balance.

I struggled to pull myself back. I was engulfed in a swirl of shadows. I was being sucked into the hole.

Was I going through?

I was going through.

I felt like I was made of light and air, not blood and bones. I felt like I was made of all the shadows who'd gone through with me. I was through and I was floating. I was weightless in the cool, damp air, drifting down slowly, swaying from side to side. Then, in an instant, they left me. I knew they'd gone because I became aware of the weight of my own body again. I felt heavy and I hurtled downwards. I slapped into water and I went under, dragged down by my body of blood and bone. I sank, and the deeper I dropped, the lighter it became and I saw the water was streaked with silver. It looked alive, like a mass of sleek, eyeless, muscly eels clustering around me, coiling around my ankles. I flapped and I kicked. I worked my arms and legs like crazy. I had to get back to the safety of air and earth. No, more than that, I had to get back to the circus. But was that even possible? And how long could I last down here?

There was nothing here except me and the river now. Even those creatures had gone, if they'd ever really been there.

Got to flow with the river, got to keep flowing higher.

Got to ride that river right back to the mire.

I could hear the boatman's voice in my head. The hypnotic rhythm caught me and, as I chanted along with it, I stopped flailing and making things worse and started to move in time with the song, and myself.

As I repeated it over and over, I knew then that if I *were* able to get back, I would have succeeded in Mother Matushka's challenge. Now I'd gone through and was no longer in the circus, wasn't I something she didn't have? There was nothing here to bring back but me.

Got to flow with the river, got to keep flowing higher.
Got to ride that river right back to the mire.

I pushed up with my mind and propelled myself through the water with my arms, using the same force I'd used to move the moon and the sun. The waters lightened and I smelled earth, and roses, and a marshy riverbank, and I wondered if that meant I was nearly there, and if that meant I had nothing to worry about, and everything to look forward to. I didn't know, but the smell was getting stronger and stronger, and I could see Mum, Dad and Daisy again, inside my head. They were holding each other, looking down on me, solemn and silent at first, until Mum broke.

'So this is it. This is it.' Mum was watching me, sobbing. I saw her turn to Daisy.

'I could have done something. I could have saved Granny. I could have stopped all this. One of Granny's daughters got in touch with her, but I tore up the letter. Only one of them died. It *is* my fault. They could have been reunited.'

Stop it, Mum. Stop it. Don't say that.

'Don't Mum,' Daisy whispered. 'We could try to find her now. Maybe she's still alive.' She hugged Mum, and I saw she was clutching her doll.

Always keep her with you, Daisy. Always keep her.

I wondered if maybe Mum would find Lilka and have her

own new big sister. She'd need looking after. All I had now was myself, and I was taking that with me, along with the news that Lilka had survived, and a desire to do all I could in the circus – to take all the auditions, to learn everything I could about Mother's work and, most of all, to learn how to do my own work.

They each kissed me and faded to nothing.

Goodbye. I love you. I love you.

I was alone.

I felt myself rise through the water.

Got to flow with the river, got to keep flowing higher.

Got to ride that river right back to the mire.

I opened my eyes and saw Mother Matushka. I was back in her cottage, back in the Circus of the Unseen.

'Well, child, you have brought yourself back. While you were gone, you were something I lacked, and now you have brought yourself back to me. Is this what you wanted?' she asked. 'Is this what you wished for?'

'I wanted to go home.' I smiled. I'd never felt such peace. I felt like my heart was glowing with light *and* blood. 'This must be home.'

Acknowledgements

To Catherine Clarke for finding Rosie a home, and to the Hot Key clan for being the best home for her, especially Sarah Odedina, Kate Manning, Georgia Murray, Holly Kyte, Jet Purdie and Ruth Logan.

To my parents, John and Joan; to Katie, Dan, Jack, Mollie and Tillie, and to James, Jesse and Lily, for being the best family.

To my husband, Stephen, for incredible support, bunches of adventures and being my best everything.

Joanne Owen

Joanne Owen was born in Pembrokeshire, Wales, and read Social and Political Sciences with Archaeology and Anthropology at St John's College, Cambridge. Now living in North London, Joanne has published two previous Young Adult novels. Steeped in the atmosphere of nineteenth-century Prague, *Puppet Master* blends the magic of marionette theatre with Czech folklore and legends. Described by the *Guardian* as 'timeless', *Puppet Master* was longlisted for the Carnegie Medal and Branford Boase award and has been translated into several languages.

Her second novel, *The Alchemist and the Angel*, is a fantastical historical epic set in sixteenth-century Prague, among the plague-ridden ghettos and decadent court of mad Emperor Rudolf. It was described by *The School Librarian* as 'an imaginative tour de force'. Follow Joanne on Facebook at www.facebook.com/JoanneOwenBooks or on Twitter: @JoanneOwen.

Thank you for choosing a Hot Key book.

If you want to know more about our authors
and what we publish, you can find us online.

You can start at our website

www.hotkeybooks.com

And you can also find us on:

We hope to see you soon!